This book is dedicated to my husband, who encourages me to follow my dream.

To my amazing friends and family for their endless support. Lastly to the reader, who stays up late, trying to finish one more chapter.

Belli Causa
Living Mountains
Janua
URBS ANTIQUA
Dark River
Dark River
Arena
CHRYSI POLI
Campis Secretum
Azraq Lake
QUAESITOR

CLAN OF THE ARCHANGEL SERIES

BOOK 2

True Spirit

GRACIE MITCHELL

True Spirit

Silva
VENTUS
AQUAM
CAPUT
Elementa
Vallis
Coal Mountains
MORTEM
N
W
E
S

Chapter 1

Elijah, Head of the Raphael Archangel Clan, sat in his office reading through the reports from other regions. He addressed all of the immediate items for his citizens. The Raphael angels in the countryside were slowly being released back to their homes, with extra security measures. Elijah received word that the largest hole in the southern regions had been shut finally, closing off the portal where most of the demons had gone through. Now fewer demon hordes overwhelmed towns. Tentatively, the citizens who lived just outside of Ventus, the capital city of his region in Silva, were safe.

Odd, he thought as he read over the last article.

How does a whole army of demons disappear? Confused, he looked over the report from Chrysi Poli again. While he compared the other messages on the 'holes' left in their realm, spirit realm, he pondered allowing some of his citizens to return home. The spirit realm was the last dimension that demons and monsters went through to reach the human world. Thus, it created a constant flow of demons and monsters breaking through their realm to obtain their food source.

Demons fed on human emotions. They possessed an insatiable appetite that drove them mad. Demons absorbed emotions and energy, most often ones of depression, anxiety, or any form of negative stress. When demons consumed these, it usually left the victim feeling drained, tired, and worse than before. Demons knew humans wouldn't notice the change, making them the preferred food source.

Humans could be saved before that point; however, the angels from the different clans already had enough to worry about. Elijah moved onto the next report, one from a team of angels in the human realm. There were angels who stayed in the human realm for years on end, catching the demons who slipped through the spirit realm. The rangers.

Or really, the misfits, he thought.

Angels sent to live with the rangers typically came from mixed clan heritage. Angels who didn't fully identify with one clan. Every year, each clan held a training seminar and competition shortly after to test the angel's ability. The competition determined the angel's uniqueness or oddity from the general population. In Elijah's region, the more the angel diverged from normal Raphael angel abilities, the more likely they would become a ranger. Raphael angels were tested for the ability to analyze, diagnose, and treat comrades without the full use of their powers. Only one winner was chosen from each region to join the rangers. Soon, Elijah would have to host another competition.

I'll also have to save up enough spiritual power to send the winner to the human realm, Elijah thought bleakly.

The amount of energy it took to go back and forth between realms was exorbitant. It often took him several days to have enough power stored up to make the trip. Only the Gabriel Clan possessed the ability to freely travel between the realms with little effort.

On that thought, Elijah pondered anxiously. He wondered how his wife was doing in Lanua. How would Charlotte handle the news? His heart twisted at the secrecy surrounding her wedding. They had planned for his sweet, youngest daughter to marry the Gabriel heir in exchange for passage to the human realm. Elijah's true goal was to find a way to get his family back. With his eldest daughter, Ava, and her children in

Sanctum, Elijah couldn't reach his daughter or grandchildren. When Mikael took Ava away, an emotional and physical door slammed in his face, blocking him out. However, now was his chance.

After Atarah married into another family, one he had influence over, then Mikael couldn't hide his daughter behind the moving mountains. At least, that was what Elijah hoped. His heart twisted at the memory of when Ava was taken. The chasm disappeared when he was close to Ava. Or around Arick and Atarah, Ava's children, for a period of time.

He sighed. He desired his family back together again. Even if that meant marrying Atarah off to another family, specifically one who had a border next to his region.

A knock on the door pulled Elijah's attention.

"Message for you, sir." A soldier entered. Based on the coloring and design of his uniform, he came from Noah's division. Sweat drenched his uniform from head to toe; his wings quivered with exhaustion.

Looks like he had a long journey from the Coal Mountains, Elijah thought.

He reached out and took the rolled-up slip of paper from the soldier.

"Is this from my son?" Elijah inquired; his brow furrowed. The paper was wrapped with a single red ribbon. Red meant urgent in their military.

"Yes, sir," the soldier stammered. "He said it was quite important."

Elijah quickly removed the ribbon and unraveled the paper. His wings flared wide as he read the first line. As Elijah read further, he stood. He moved from his chair and around his large, oak desk.

"Soldier," Elijah said distantly, still reading.

"Yes...sir?"

"Call in the royal council immediately, and tell them to take over the paperwork for now."

"Yes, sir," the soldier sputtered once more. "Right away, sir." The soldier scurried out of the room.

The slip of paper dropped from Elijah's hands and onto the floor.

I need to get to Lanua immediately. There's a halfling on the loose! My wife and children are in danger!

Chapter 2

Atarah watched the horizon over the city. Cars and people moved about, continuing their daily lives. Unaware of their presence. *At least for the moment,* Atarah thought grimly.

A rustling noise alerted her to someone's approach. She tensed for a moment before relaxing as she heard Charlotte's soft footsteps. Without the serum, her powers and her wings were on full display.

Charlotte stepped around the trees that covered her. The setting sunlight beamed across her face, showcasing her hazel eyes. Her elegant face bore no signs of tears today. Her wings remained relaxed, while her face showed concern. They both still wore clothing from Chrysi Poli, more like rags now after the fight with the Abaddon. The worry on Charlotte's face disappeared as her eyes found Atarah.

She sat down by Atarah's side and silently put her head on her shoulder. Atarah leaned in closer.

Her best friend—no, sister more like.

Since Gabriel Jr. had trapped them in the human realm, over the past few days, Atarah and Charlotte had become closer than ever. Atarah rarely left Charlotte's side, and Charlotte rarely left her side. Not out of fear, but out of companionship and healing. Atarah suspected Charlotte sought comfort after learning of her mother's betrayal. Her mother, Elizabeth, schemed for Atarah and Charlotte to be married off into other clans. She planned Atarah's marriage out of revenge against her father, but Charlotte... Charlotte's marriage was more like a payment. Not love. Collateral damage.

The sting of Elizabeth's betrayal lingered. Nonetheless, Elizabeth's plot was not a complete surprise. They both knew Elizabeth possessed hatred in her heart for Atarah and her father. The true reason Atarah sought Charlotte's company was because of Ben's betrayal. Ben's deception was a dagger through her heart compared to Elizabeth's little sting. A dagger that twisted each time she thought of his name.

Atarah clenched a hand to her chest as it constricted around her. The pain had not lessened, not even the slightest bit, since they had been trapped in the human realm. Her wings trembled and slumped to the ground. *It is getting harder to breathe,* Atarah thought as she tried to relax. A darkness started in the corner of her eye and closed in. Slowly creeping in until the gloom became part of her. Once the darkness altered her, the void grew. She was not sure what was worse. The crippling pain of betrayal or this emptiness inside her.

Charlotte encircled her into a big hug as if sensing the chasm within her. With her ivory wings, she encapsulated them. Her hands glowed slightly as she attempted to use her powers again, but in vain. No matter how much she tried, her healing hands did nothing for Atarah's broken heart.

The hug does help, though, Atarah thought.

Charlotte's embrace helped her stay together, instead of falling apart. Atarah wrapped her arms around Charlotte's trembling form. She tightened her hold. They held each other. Or else they would both fall to pieces.

The sun hit the horizon with a tremendous, pink glow falling across the sky. In the distance, darkness closed in on the setting sun as if chasing it away. The night promised a change, a transformation. Slowly, as the sun faded, Atarah noticed her breathing became more regular, and her wings stopped trembling. A numbing, tingling sensation spread throughout her body as the darkness within her promised its own change and transformation.

Rustling leaves startled Charlotte, but not Atarah. She constantly used her powers now, her ability to expand her senses. To see, hear, and feel everything around her, dead or living. Or really to see if one angel in particular was around her. She didn't care when her head ached at such prolonged use. She needed to know when Ben crept toward the spot they sat minutes ago. He hesitantly peeked around the tree branch he hid behind. Though she did not have his gift of mind reading, she could tell he was anxious.

Gabriel was several meters back, ducking behind a tree to see if Ben would be thrown back or not. Gabriel and Ben had mostly kept their distance from her and Charlotte. If they ventured too close, Atarah would expand her strength outwardly and try to crush them. The only time they ventured closer to them was during nightfall.

On the first day, Atarah tried to crush Gabriel into taking them back into the Spirit realm; however, it was to no avail. Gabriel refused to go against any orders from his father. His father's orders being, 'Stay in the human realm until I give the signal to come back.' Not satisfied with this, Atarah tried to beat him into taking them back. Again, with no success. Gabriel ground his teeth and bore every punch and kick Atarah gave him. Not even fighting back against her. Or defending himself against her attacks.

Ben tried to stop her, but every time their eyes met, he flinched as if she had punched him instead of Gabriel. Eventually, she became too exhausted from pummeling Gabriel and gave up entirely. All she could do now was wait. Her worst nightmare, waiting on someone else's role to play. Whether it be her father, brother, or Gabriel, she had to depend on them to get out of the human realm.

Now Ben and Gabriel came toward them cautiously as if she would snap at them any minute. Charlotte's eyes shifted from Ben's crouched form to Gabriel. Their eyes met briefly before she dropped her gaze and snuggled closer to Atarah. Gabriel's gaze turned to the ground in shame. Neither Atarah nor Charlotte had spoken to the men since the first day. Now that five days had passed, it was time to talk to them.

Not to reconcile, but to create a better plan.

Even though they were in the human realm, that did not mean there were no demons. Nor did it mean they were the only angels.

"Gabriel. B-Be-Selaphiel," Atarah called out to them.

They both froze, surprised. Charlotte's wings flared when they came close. Gabriel glanced at Ben, raising his eyebrow, silently asking if he knew anything. Ben shrugged. He had explained once that he could not hear the exact thought, but he could decipher the overall gist of what someone thought and felt.

"I think it is time we talk about what is to come next," Atarah spoke, her tone hard. Gabriel's wings flared out of instinctual defense. Ben winced while his wings slumped. They both came forward nonetheless. Gabriel looked warily at Ben before speaking.

"Decided to speak to us again, huh? Without throwing a tantrum. I am impressed," Gabriel goaded.

His right eye was still black, along with a good size bruise on his chin. His wings trembled, despite his attempted bravado. Atarah stared at him, feeling nothing. His eyes shifted back and forth across her face, unsure.

"We cannot keep hiding in these woods forever. Eventually, demons will sense us and come to attack us," Atarah spoke calmly and clearly.

"Where would we go?" Charlotte asked, her brows furrowed with worry. "We don't have any serum."

Humans were not allowed to see spiritual beings. Everyone followed this rule no matter what. Even demons.

"We need to find the rangers," Atarah responded.

They all looked at her skeptically. The rangers were like

a distant relative you heard about, but never saw or interacted with, except for a few rare holidays. Rangers did not care if you were from a different house or clan from their own. Once you were part of their crew, you were equal with everyone. They despised hierarchy of any kind. The rangers rolled their eyes and scoffed at the Archangels back in the Spirit realm.

Considering they were heirs of the Archangel Houses, Atarah expected some hesitation. After all, they represented what the rangers hated about life in the Spirit realm.

"Would they even be willing to help us?" Ben asked in a soft voice.

Atarah answered honestly, "I am not sure. However, I would be shocked if they would turn us away in our current state. We have no serum and there are demons here."

Disliking them was a strong possibility, but turning them away was an even stronger impossibility. No matter what, they would come to their aid if a demon attacked them. She needed to use that to their advantage.

"All we have to do is follow the demons. Demons follow humans, and the rangers follow the demons."

"How will we follow them without being seen?" Gabriel asked with flared wings.

He sounds frustrated with my idea, Atarah mused.

"We move at night, when most humans are asleep and demons are active," Atarah replied. "We cover ourselves as much as possible with whatever we can find. Blankets, clothes, sheets, anything. We hover around the edge of the town down below and wait for the demons to start hunting."

"How do we know the rangers will come?" Charlotte asked, still skeptical.

"I have faith they will be there," Atarah said in a gentle tone.

Charlotte's wings relaxed. She would follow Atarah's plan. That was all that truly mattered.

She turned to Gabriel and Ben. She could care less if they

joined or not, but she'd rather know. For if they were going to come along, she may need to adjust her plan. Out of the corner of her eye, she saw Ben flinch again as if he had been hit. His wings slumped around him.

She looked at him with dead eyes. He winced again.

"I will go with whatever you decide," Ben replied softly.

Gabriel watched Ben with sympathy before answering Atarah. "I will go as well," he replied with a nod.

"Very well," Atarah said. "It is all agreed on."

Atarah slowly stood. Charlotte followed her movement. Gabriel's eyes immediately went to Charlotte as she moved.

He took a half step toward her as if to help her up. However, he appeared to think better of it when Charlotte tensed. Atarah's wings flared out. If Charlotte didn't want him near, she would make sure he didn't get too close. As he looked between the two of them, Gabriel's wings dipped.

Nonetheless, a spark entered his eyes as he looked at Charlotte, as if saying he was not going to give up.

"Let's fly down there." Atarah pointed to the town in the distance.

Lights came on in a few spots throughout the town, giving it some illumination in the darkness.

"Stay low, hide behind whatever building you can, and keep watch," Atarah told everyone. She whispered to Charlotte, "Stay close."

Charlotte gave a nod before opening up her wings and lifting off into the sky. Atarah took off right after her, followed by Ben and Gabriel. Atarah flew past Charlotte and dove down the hill they had been stranded on. She pulled up at the last second, gliding just above the ground.

The town was not far, and it was small. She didn't know where they were in the human world, but it mattered very little. She was oddly grateful that Gabriel had not transported them to a ridiculously large city like Paris, New York City, or Tokyo. Considering the forest surrounding them, they appeared to be in a rural area. Nature somehow looked duller in the human world. Not enough vibrance compared to the Spirit realm. The area around the town was flat, with crops for a few miles until the mountains began to encroach. The buildings were low to the ground and no higher than a story or two tall. Some roads were paved, while others were gravel.

Despite having lights, the town appeared dim. Many dark corners and alleyways provided coverage. Perfect for them. She landed softly on the rooftop of an old building on the edge of town. There was little light on this side of town, which worked in their favor. She expanded her senses all across the city to sense everything. She heard all the humans who moved and slept. She felt the vibrations of the footsteps of those who wandered. She smelled the exhaust from all the cars driving within the town. She knew exactly where everyone was. This was the perfect spot for them to pick out demons.

"Are we safe?" Charlotte whispered behind her.

While Atarah had scanned the area, everyone had landed on the rooftop.

They all crouched with their wings tucked in as tightly as possible. They attempted to hide their wings so humans could not spot them.

"We are safe," Atarah spoke at a normal volume. "There are no humans in the building beneath us."

They stood from their cowarded positions. Their wings relaxed away from their shoulders.

"Well, that's a relief." Gabriel sighed. "How long do we have to stay up here?" He directed his question to Atarah.

"Until we find a demon to track, of course," Atarah replied cynically.

Gabriel's eyes narrowed at her tone, but she didn't care. She turned her attention back to the small town before them.

It is quite unremarkable, Atarah thought. She expanded her senses again to search for demons.

She closed her eyes and waited. She concentrated on the

forms and energies of every moving creature. She directed her focus on the energy of malice, deception, or manipulation. Her own spirit remained calm and undisturbed. She opened her eyes.

"Any luck finding demons?" Gabriel asked sarcastically. His arms crossed on his chest, and a single eyebrow raised.

Atarah pursed her lips. "Not yet."

She turned back to the town. How was it that this town did not have a single demon? Did they need to move closer to an urban area? That would increase their risk of exposure. A bigger area meant more humans; which would attract more demons.

Atarah closed her eyes and tried again. Gabriel paced around the rooftop, frustrated, as he waited for Atarah.

Atarah pursed her lips. "Not yet."

She turned back to the town. How was it that this town did not have a single demon? Did they need to move closer to an urban area? That would increase their risk of exposure. A bigger area meant more humans; which would attract more demons.

Atarah closed her eyes and tried again.

Gabriel paced around the rooftop, frustrated, as he waited for Atarah. With each hour they waited, his irritation grew. He purposely chose the outskirts of this town because of the limited demon activity. He doubted any demon or even any *rangers* for that matter would be close. He debated breaking the news to Atarah, but one glance at Charlotte made him pause. One of her soft curls came out of place and toward her eyes. Her stunning, hazel eyes. The shine of them enraptured Gabriel. They always had, for years. His chest tightened as he gazed at her.

In his earlier years, he had hoped and prayed for a natural

encounter, an excuse to talk to her. After the months went by and nothing happened, he thought he'd take matters into his own hands. Determined to get his feelings across, he walked over to her and… froze. The moment her gorgeous eyes connected with his, he completely stopped. Gabriel cringed at the memory. He couldn't even get his name out! Or say hello! Instead, he stared at her like a creep, turned bright red, and scampered away. He might have screamed into his pillow that night in horror at his own awkwardness, but he shook the memory away.

Shortly after that embarrassing attempt, Mikael decided to steal Charlotte's older sister and locked her away. He had only been a young angel back then, no more than eight, so he hardly thought much of the incident until it turned the Raphael Clan crazy with suspicion of the other clans. They hid themselves away, including Charlotte. Dashing any hopes Gabriel had to talk to her again.

He complained for months to his mother about his aching heart. However, she laughed off his declaration of love as nothing more than a childhood crush. One day, he would be the Clan Head, and he had prayed Charlotte didn't marry in the meantime. As the years passed, he trained, practiced, and studied as much as he could. His father joked that he studied as much as a Raziel angel. He wanted to grow, to better himself out of the stammering fool he had been. So, training and studying was how he spent his time. Between his tutors and his family, Gabriel hardly interacted with anyone his own age as he grew up. Though this, he did mind. His awkwardness was not only with Charlotte—though it was definitely worse with her—but his social ineptitude was the reason he kept to himself growing up.

He followed his father around as much as he would allow. His father was always so sure of himself. Always knew what to do. Admiration was too little of a word to describe what his father meant to him. He practically worshiped him.

He stood tall and knew how to anticipate what to do next. Gabriel wanted to lead like him when he became the Head of the Gabriel Clan.

Then, on the fateful day of the emergency summit meeting in the human realm, Gabriel's heart stirred once more. She sat there, even more beautiful than when he first met her. Gabriel went rigid with nervousness. So much so, he grew scared to talk to her again. His mother noticed, of course, much to his embarrassment. She had asked him afterward, in front of his father, if he still had feelings for her.

"Yes," he had said defeatedly.

He talked in detail of how his stomach filled with knots when he was around her. How light he felt on his feet, and how conscious he became of how he looked, dressed, and stood. How embarrassed he was when he couldn't even introduce himself! He spilled it all to his mother and father. Never in his life would he have done that if he had known. He regretted it with all his being.

He never knew his parents would scheme a marriage for his sake. It wasn't until the day before the wedding that they told him their plan. Gabriel had never gone against his father's orders because he had faith in him. However, that day was the first time Gabriel almost disobeyed him. The way poor Charlotte trembled in his arms struck him through the heart. Gabriel had not—no, he *could not*—forget. Her body, weak from exhaustion, should have passed out from the harsh trek. Not Charlotte. Her concern for her friend kept her awake and fighting. Gabriel's feelings for her grew from that alone.

Gabriel shook his head and pulled out of his memory. Charlotte looked away from him. He paced again in the opposite direction, even more frustrated with himself than anyone else. Now his worst nightmare had come true! Charlotte despised him. She cringed away from him as if he were a halfling.

He sighed, knowing he deserved such treatment. *Please,*

he prayed, *let me fix this in some way.* He wanted something, anything, better than this. Even if they were only friends and nothing more. He continued pacing, trying to think of a way to mend what was between him and Charlotte. While in his thoughts, he had paced closer and closer to where Charlotte sat, unconsciously. He didn't notice until Charlotte's wings flared, alerting Atarah, whom Gabriel didn't see coming.

Suddenly, a force pushed him. His legs swept up from under him, causing him to fall flat on his back. He waited for the pain, but none came. He sat up to see a faint glow from Charlotte's eyes and hand, the glow of her powers. His heart soared. He knew they were nowhere near friends, but hope bloomed anyway. She had healed him once before. The day when Atarah went crazy trying to force him to send them back to the Spirit realm. If Charlotte hadn't healed his injuries so quickly, he would have been hobbling around. Hope, *damn hope*, spread like the warmth from her healing touch. His chest felt warm, and his wings hummed.

Charlotte looked away from him. Atarah relaxed her posture once Charlotte did.

Even though he knew why Atarah acted out, Gabriel still vented his frustration.

"What did you do that for?" he cried out.

"You spooked Charlotte." Atarah turned back to the small town and ignored him once more.

"I don't think that warrants a knock down," Gabriel grumbled.

He gave a shy glance to Charlotte. Despite her calm, almost bored demeanor, her wings were tense, portraying her true feelings.

"Here."

Ben stood to Gabriel's left, offering his hand in assistance. Gabriel accepted the help. Gabriel pitied Ben almost as much as he did himself. Since they'd arrived, Ben's eyes had sunken in, his wings drooped, and he constantly gazed at Atarah longingly. Gabriel felt true empathy for Ben. To have someone you love right before you and yet so far away. A cruel fate. Ben's predicament was crueler at times. Every now and then, due to Ben's power, he winced or recoiled from hearing Atarah's thoughts. At least Gabriel could ignorantly hope to earn Charlotte's trust back, while Ben heard the loss of trust with Atarah.

"Are you going to tell them?" Ben whispered to Gabriel. Of course, Ben knew his dilemma.

"I am trying to think of a way to bring it up," Gabriel replied softly, but it was not quiet enough.

"Bring what up?" Charlotte's voice pierced the very air around him.

He turned to find her looking at him. He froze and his wings began to tremble. "I… I… err… ha… What?" he muttered stupidly.

"What were you talking about with Ben?" Charlotte asked gently. Her wings were more relaxed this time.

"We… I… were just talking about…" Gabriel stammered. He hadn't thought of a good answer yet.

Mercifully, Atarah drew everyone's attention.

"I sense a demon coming this way," Atarah said in a low voice, but loud enough for everyone to hear.

Charlotte's wings flared back up in fear at the mention of demons. Gabriel moved closer to her, wanting to protect her. How did a demon come here? He didn't want any demons near Charlotte.

"What? How?" Gabriel asked, shocked.

"I don't know," Atarah muttered. "It is coming from this side of the town and fast." She pointed to the side of town they had flown in from.

They all crouched down low on the rooftop.

"We are in luck," Ben said after a few minutes. "Its thoughts are not on us, but on humans. It's come to feed."

"What kind of demon is it?" Charlotte asked, looking between Ben and Atarah.

She shivered. Gabriel inched closer and expanded one of his black, feathery wings, so the wind would no longer blow on her.

"I can't tell," Atarah said, her brows furrowed in concentration.

"I don't think you would be able to," Gabriel explained. "Demons can change their forms in the human realm, so it would be difficult to pinpoint what kind of demon it was from a distance."

"Do you really think a ranger will come?" Charlotte directed her question to Atarah.

Her eyes shined with hope. Gabriel's heart clenched. His father had never said anything against meeting up with the rangers. He thought, *Maybe I could help…*

"We will find a ranger," Gabriel said, answering Charlotte's question with more confidence than he expected.

Charlotte turned to him. Her eyes widened briefly, noticing how close he was, but otherwise did not look alarmed. "What do you mean?" Charlotte asked. Her eyes narrowed in on him in distrust.

"Well… I can… I can... help," Gabriel murmured.

Come on, angel up! Don't be a fairy! he thought.

"If worse comes to worst," Gabriel started, "I can transport us closer to the rangers. My powers can work in the Spirit realm and human realm, but… I—"

"You don't know where the rangers are?" Atarah finished for him, eyeing Gabriel.

Gabriel grimaced. "Their base is always moving. They don't like to give out their location either, for demons have hunted them for millennia," Gabriel answered.

"Why are you telling us this now? And not before?" Charlotte asked, suspicion rising in her voice.

Gabriel paused. He hadn't thought of this.

"Never mind, Charlotte," Atarah whispered, looking toward the hills they flew from. "The demon is arriving. Stay quiet and out of sight. We will follow it and intervene only when needed."

A dark figure crawled into view as it moved closer to the lights of the town. Its torso was big and black, while the neck was abnormally long. Despite its black body, the neck and face were pale. The face was narrow and sharp with no nose or any visible mouth. It had small, pale, glazed over eyes that appeared to stare at nothing. The figure was so still, Gabriel would have thought it to be a scarecrow. Slowly, the demon moved, revealing long, dangly arms. It wore nothing except a scrap of clothing around its torso. To call it even a scrap of clothing was generous. The demon's arms and legs were covered in cuts and scars.

Suddenly, the demon contorted itself. Sounds of crackling and bones snapping so loudly, they could hear it from where they hid. Gabriel covered his mouth as he tried not to gag at the way the demon's body writhed. The demon's arms snapped in half, while the face began to bubble. Unable to take anymore, Gabriel looked away, but he couldn't escape the horrific sounds.

Something landed on his shoulder. He turned to see Charlotte's hand on his shoulder, slightly aglow to help with the nausea. She still watched the demon, down below. With his stomach more stable, he braved another look at the demon. However, what he saw marveled him. On the ground, there no longer stood a deformed, frightening creature, but… a normal human. He knew demons could change their appearances when they entered the human realm, but he had not witnessed their mastery of this power firsthand.

The demon had settled on an average human height, a sturdy build, and plain-looking features. Not a face to remember in a crowd. The only thing that could give away what was hidden underneath were its dark, empty eyes.

It began to move, awkwardly at first, as if getting used

to its new body. By the time the demon reached one of the streets, it walked normally. It strolled along the side of the building and onto the main streets. It stepped from the main street, turned onto another street and out of their sight.

They all released a sigh of relief. Atarah moved first. She stood from their crouched hiding spot and leaned over the ledge.

"We have to follow it," she stated, looking at where they had last seen the creature.

"How exactly do you plan on doing that?" Gabriel asked sarcastically. "That thing can blend in. Without the serum, we stick out like a sore thumb!"

Atarah grinned mischievously at him. "We're gonna go rooftop hopping."

Without another word, Atarah sprinted full speed to the other end of the rooftop. When she reached the edge, she took a ridiculously large jump, catapulting herself onto the next building in front of them. Gabriel quickly glanced toward the street to see if any humans saw her. There were none on the street. No cars drove by either. Gabriel looked up to see Atarah waving at them to jump.

Gabriel scoffed. He often forgot she was a Michael Angel, then she did something physically impossible. Ben didn't hesitate to follow her. He opened up his wings and silently glided across the street to join her. Charlotte didn't appear deterred either. She glanced both ways on the street before opening up her wings and gliding across. Gabriel looked hesitantly back toward the hill where they had remained for days. There was no going back now.

He opened his black wings and flew across.

Chapter 3

Mikael pinched his eyebrows together in concentration as he gathered and stored his power within himself. The conscious effort proved to be difficult and required much focus. It was like fixating on one's breathing and holding on to every bit of oxygen. Pulling it within the body to store it within his muscles. However, instead of oxygen, it was his spiritual power.

After receiving the message from Arick, Mikael immediately began gathering his power. He thought through his own plan of action to bring his daughter back. Stationed within Quaesitor city library for days, Mikael planned out his next few moves with Joshua.

He knew his daughter could handle herself in the human world; however, what worried him were the other angels around her. After hearing additional reports, he knew there were two battles he'd have to face: getting his daughter back and handling the Abaddon.

Mikael's stomach clenched. He could not believe his daughter faced an Abaddon and lived. Through reported sightings, they attempted to track the Abaddon after Atarah fought it. He never forgot his first time fighting an Abaddon, back when Matthew was alive. If his older brother Matthew had not been there, Mikael would have died. Mikael's heart ached, thinking of his brother.

His brother died a long time ago. The 'Matthew' who plagued his life now, a Luciferian, slithered around in the demon realm, plotting his next move. Meanwhile, Mikael had to turn his attention to finding the Abaddon lurking in their realm. Mikael sighed. The heaviness of all that he must do weighted him down in spirit. He needed another one of himself to accomplish everything on his to-do list. A knock on the door distracted him mercifully.

"Come in," Mikael commanded gruffly.

The door opened slowly to reveal Arick. The heavy weight upon him lightened upon seeing his son; however, it was short lived. Arick's eyes appeared withdrawn, and his wings dragged on the floor. After learning his true parentage, Arick was not doing well. Since traveling back from Lanua, Arick had refused all food and company, except for large amounts of alcohol. Noah, the Raphael heir, attempted numerous times to convince Arick to leave his room, but to no avail. Surprised to see him, Mikael thought his next mission was the step in the right direction.

Mikael's hopes faltered a little by the hollow look in his son's eyes. Arick looked haggard, as if he had not showered in days. His black shirt with the family insignia looked ripped apart, while his pants were severely wrinkled. His hair was tousled and unkempt. Arick appeared somber and grim.

"What is it, son?" Mikael asked.

Arick's wings flinched at the word 'son.' No sarcastic reply or smirk. *Very concerning,* Mikael thought. Arick closed the door and walked toward the desk where Mikael sat. Papers scattered across the light-colored, clay desk, each giving reports from all across the regions. Arick glanced down at the map of the region before answering.

"Noah received an update from his father, Elijah, today," Arick answered. His voice sounded raspy as if this was the first time he had used it in days.

"What was the update?" Mikael asked. He stood from his chair and moved closer to Arick. Arick's wings flared at his approach, but Mikael ignored it.

"The angels of Sanctum have retreated to Silva. Elijah is housing them until the Abaddon can be found and killed."

"That is good." Mikael sighed in relief. "With our people safe now, we can move onto the next step."

Arick leaned across the table and picked up a piece of paper. It was a report from Chrysi Poli. The army of demons had disappeared.

"Oh," Arick said, detached. "And what is that next step?" he asked as if bored.

Mikael grabbed the piece of paper from Arick. "Do not worry about that right now," Mikael said gruffly. "Look at me, Arick."

Arick kept his gaze down, wings flared, and face expressionless. Mikael's wings stayed relaxed.

"Arick," Mikael said in a tougher, commanding tone.

Arick's wings twitched, and his eyes came alive with anger. Arick whirled on Mikael. His hands curled into fists with a look in his eye conveying he wanted to fight. Oddly, this comforted Mikael. He wanted his son to keep fighting, never to give up, never to succumb.

Mikael placed both hands on Arick's shoulders firmly. Mikael rarely had to use all his strength, but given Arick's age and size, it was necessary.

"I know this is hard for you," Mikael said roughly. "I know you hate this, but you have to stay focused and keep moving."

Arick's jaw tightened and the fire in his eyes grew, but his wings shook.

"I need your help, Arick," Mikael said more gently. Arick's wings calmed slightly. "I have to stay here and keep everyone safe from the Abaddon. But I need you to retrieve your sister from the human realm and come home with her." Mikael looked hard into Arick's eyes. "For what is to come... I need everyone to fight, especially you and your sister."

Arick tried to step away, but Mikael held firm.

"Let go of me," Arick said in a soft yet hard tone. "I need… space away from *you*."

Mikael's heart clenched at his son's words. He knew Arick was hurting and wished there was something he could do for him. Mikael released his grip, but his wings came up around them.

"Space I can give, however much you'd like," Mikael said. Arick's eyes were still ablaze with anger. "But isolation I will not give you, son."

Mikael glanced sideways at the door. He could see the shadows of a couple of feet shuffled underneath the door frame.

"I am not the only one with this sentiment either." Mikael lowered his wings and walked back around the desk.

"I have gathered up enough power to open up the divide between our realm and the human realm. You and whoever you choose will go to the human realm and bring Atarah"— Mikael paused, grinning at the door once more—"and Charlotte back to our realm, safely and soundly."

The feet at the door froze. Arick glanced at the entrance , confused by Mikael's glance.

"Choose wisely, son." Mikael drew Arick's attention back to him. "You leave tonight with your team. Be safe. Don't forget the techniques I showed you, and seek out the ranger Luke. He's a bit…" Mikael grinned. "He's a bit odd, but in his heart of hearts, he is good."

Arick's wings were still flared, and his fists clenched, but he gave a nod anyway. Arick turned toward the door to walk out. The feet behind the door scurried away.

"Oh, and Arick," Mikael called out. Arick stopped at the door, but did not turn around. "No matter what happens, I am on your side."

Arick's wings flinched again. Without a backward glance, he left the study.

Arick struggled and failed to control his anger as he shut the door to his father's temporary study. The anger came on so strong and overwhelming, it shook his whole body, trying to look for a way out. Not wanting to explode again, he walked down the hall, not caring where he ended up, as long as he was alone. He wished he could go numb again. He needed a drink.

Alone with his thoughts, Arick thought back to nearly a week ago. After Gabriel Jr. had transported his sister, Charlotte, and Ben to the human realm, Arick had stood there stunned for a few minutes. He stared at the empty space where his sister had been, while chaos ensued. Brock, Galvin, and Jared fought off the guards of the Gabriel Clan, while Rachael and Elizabeth tried to make a run for it. However, at that time, so much anger came crashing down onto him, he couldn't move for a moment.

One moment, he was standing still, the next, an enormous amount of power shot out from him. He never felt so out of touch with his own body, never so out of control. His power shot out and slammed into everyone around him. All the guards were knocked down. Gabriel Sr., Head Archangel of the clan, could not stand. Even his own team—Brock, Jared, and Galvin—withered on the ground in agony over the amount of force Arick had brought down upon them. A sonic blast of sorts ricocheted around the entire estate.

The balcony he stood on broke and cracked under the weight of his power. The city quaked over the effects of Arick's strength. Tariel was the one who saved them all and helped Arick regain control. She came up behind him and gently placed her hand on his shoulder. She used her powers to weaken Arick. Slowly, Arick reclaimed control as his powers drained away. Gradually, the force of his powers lifted from everyone on the balcony and city. Arick would never forget the glances of terror from the angels in Urbs Antiqua. Even Gabriel Sr. looked at Arick differently.

After some interrogation, it was easy to put together the pieces of Elijah and Elizabeth's plan. Marry Atarah off to another Arch House and send her as far away as they could. Revenge against Mikael for what he did to their daughter. Arick learned the truth of what happened between his parents. Not only that, but his father wasn't even his real father. His father was a demon. *A Luciferian.* The worst of the worst kinds of life form. An Archangel overrun with so much darkness for a long period of time that the angel transformed into a Luciferian. He was the spawn of pure evil.

Arick shook his head violently to rid himself of this disgust. Damn, he wished he could get drunk again. He looked up to see where he had wandered. He had walked aimlessly, stuck in his own thoughts. He hadn't paid attention to his whereabouts. He had ventured up a mountain path just outside of the city center. Many angels avoided him now. Whether out of fear or disgust, he wasn't sure. He must've hiked for miles up the mountain in complete oblivion. Before him was the end of the trail overlooking a stunning view of the city across the crystal blue lake. At the edge of the trail, Tariel sat on a stone bench gazing at the city of Quaesitor.

Tariel turned to see Arick as he approached, as if expecting him. Arick debated turning around until Tariel lifted a hand in greetings.

"It appears you wandered off," Tariel said teasingly.

"I was searching for something," Arick replied, coming to stand beside her.

For a moment, Arick took in the gorgeous view of the city and blue lake. It made him miss his own home. *That's not your home anymore*, a voice in the back of his mind whispered. His wings flared.

Tariel continued to watch him. Arick gave a half-shrug.

"I've had a lot on my mind lately."

"I've observed," Tariel replied, still looking at Arick. "And I see so much turmoil within you."

Arick shifted on his feet.

"Observed?" Arick asked.

He glanced at Tariel. Her long, navy hair seemed to absorb the sunlight that hit it, creating almost an eclipsed look around her. Seven days had passed since the disaster in Lanua. Ever since then, Tariel's presence was the only one that was... tolerable. He realized now how many times he sought her out in search of calm. Tariel gave the tiniest of grins and nodded. She was a woman of few words; that comforted Arick. He sat on the bench next to her. She no longer blushed every time their eyes met, but her wings still fluttered when he sat down. His large, black wings next to her small, pale, leathery wings created quite the contrast. But, for the first time all day, Arick rested his wings. Fully relaxed.

"You pay attention more than most, Tariel." Arick leaned forward with his elbows on his knees.

"I pay just enough," Tariel said softly.

Arick looked to the city before speaking.

"Noah and the others," Arick paused, "have been hammering at my door every day now. He always asks me to meet him in the library, but"—he rubbed his face—"I can't face them yet."

Tariel glanced at him, waiting, with no judgment.

"My anger becomes so much..." Arick struggled to get the words out. The image of the destruction in his room entered his mind. "I fear I can no longer control my own power. That's why I saw my father. I wanted to see if I had control yet. If I lost control, he would at least be there to stop me."

"A test?" Tariel asked.

"That man has frustrated me my whole life," Arick answered. "And I didn't explode, even though I wanted to. I had control, but, in that moment, I didn't want control." Arick glanced at her. "But I am hoping this means I can control my anger enough to be around others," Arick whispered the last part.

He recognized the shame at his own anger, for it confirmed he was a monster. He grew even more angry at himself. Arick ran a hand through his hair roughly, tugging out several strands. His hands shook. He clenched them tightly, afraid that he would hit something, or worse… someone. After a few moments, that didn't work. His vision began to turn red. His wings flared and vibrated. Arick held his breath and willed himself not to explode again.

Tariel placed her hand on Arick's right hand. Quickly, his power and rage dissipated. His energy levels dropped as well, but Arick didn't mind. Right now, he was grateful none of his power oozed out. Whether it be his rage or strength that left, he didn't hurt anyone else.

Zewal had once explained how the powers in the Azrael Clan worked. There were three different types of Azrael angels—ones who possessed the ability to drain a being of their energy, others with the ability to drain a being of their power, or the deadliest of the powers, an angel with the ability to drain someone of their life force. Those of high rank, like Zewal and Tariel, usually possessed one or two of the abilities. While the Archangel Head, Sewall, possessed all three abilities.

Zewal inherited the ability to drain others of their life force, while Tariel controlled two powers—the ability to drain others of their energy and power. When an Azrael angel used their powers, their victims experience severe torment, which was why they were nicknamed the angels of death. However, for Arick, Tariel using her powers felt like relief. A release of built-up pressure.

Tariel removed her hand from his. Her face remained tranquil, never taking her eyes off the city. She didn't drained him completely, only enough to keep the rage from boiling over.

"Thank you," Arick murmured.

"Do not let the sun go down on your anger," Tariel replied softly.

Arick understood what she meant. The dangers of night-time, his urge to get drunk, demons roaming about, and unchecked rage, were never a good combination. Also, it was wise to not go to sleep in anger. He knew he couldn't keep relying on Tariel nor keep stalling for what he needed to do for tonight. He stood up gingerly, so his wings would not disturb Tariel. He opened his wings and jumped off the cliff they stood on. The wind roared in his ears as he descended. He opened his wings out wide just before hitting the ground to glide above it. He flapped his wings hard and soared up to the sky.

An airstream carried Arick up as the sun bore down on his back. Arick made a large curve around the Azraq lake and started to descend into the city. The walls were now completely repaired, thanks to the extra hands of the soldiers his father had provided. The city no longer looked under siege. All remnants of the demon hordes disappeared. Arick landed upon the main gate, which now stayed open. Groups of angels gathered there with their families, packing their bags for the voyage home. Only a sparse number of demons roamed, allowing the citizens to return to their homes in the countryside.

Arick watched as the families left through the main gate. The anger started to swell up again within him as he saw their disdain. The angels of Quaesitor knew of his heritage and were disgusted with him. It was only because of Joshua's command to leave him be that he walked freely. Or else he would have been attacked or locked away... At least for now. He shook his head and tried to focus on tonight.

He moved quickly toward the Head Tree. The burgundy tree stood out against the onyx stone that surrounded it. Most of the city was carved out of the stone from the mountains, but where Arick sought laid behind the Head Tree—the City Hall. The Hall housed the largest and most mysterious library in all the realms. Arick had no doubt that he would find his ragtag team there.

Ignoring the stares, he walked up the massive stone stairs into the library. The building, carved from the black mineral, made light a necessity. Lanterns and candles placed all along the walls and desk gave as much illumination as possible. Arick grabbed a lantern of his own and started his search. He circled around the Great Hole that dove down so deep no angel had been to the bottom. The hole, lined with books all the way down, or at least everyone assumed all the way, laid in the center. Every book was cryptic and confusing, but held a wealth of knowledge that had tipped the scales in wars before.

He spotted his crew just along the edge of the Great Hole. Brock, Jared, and Galvin all stood hesitantly by the gate, looking down at the descending library. Arick's heart softened at the sight of his companions. Despite everything, all the rage and outbursts, none of them had left his side. Brock and Jared stayed persistent. Every day, they banged on his bedroom door, trying to convince him to come out to train, eat or anything. Galvin couldn't talk, but Arick sensed him outside the door. He never knocked on the door either. Simply sat outside the door in silence and waited for him. None of them blamed him, not once.

Galvin spotted him first as he approached them. Galvin's wings hummed, though nothing changed outwardly on his face. His black, nearly blueish hair blended in with the library background, making his pale face stick out even more. His dark brown eyes locked onto Arick with warmth. Galvin was an angel of mixed heritage, which was not common. His father was an Azrael angel and his mother a Raphael angel.

Everyone from his team had mixed heritage, including himself. Brock and Jared were descendants of Raphael and Gabriel angels. However, because the Raphael traits expressed more in all of them, they all grew up along the borders of Silva. Brock and Jared had stockier builds, brown hair, and ivory wings. They all were, in their own way, outcasts. Either region would have accepted them, but none of the regions would see them as fully Raphael, Azrael, or Gabriel angels. He couldn't ask for a better team.

Brock and Jared turned their heads when Galvin's wings hummed in happiness. Their own wings opened up and hummed too. Unlike Galvin, Brock and Jared both smiled and broke out into cheers upon seeing Arick. Arick grinned then.

"Come on!" Brock bellowed. "Bring it in, tough guy!"

Arick chuckled as Brock and Jared tackled him into a tight hug. Galvin stayed back, but appeared very happy. Several Raziel angels gave them irritated looks and a few told them to shush, but none of them cared. Arick felt forgiven before he had a chance to apologize to them. What little anger had built up within him dissipated. He made the right choice coming to see them.

"I…" Arick started as Brock and Jared backed away. "I do not know what to say—"

Brock waved a hand at Arick, stopping him.

"Hey now, none of this mushy stuff," Brock said.

"You had us waiting long enough, ya prick." Jared chuckled.

"Yeah!" Brock jumped in. "You Archs are such drama queens. Us regular angels don't know how to deal with the tantrums you throw."

Brock and Jared laughed, and even Galvin quietly chuckled. A shuffle sound caught Arick's attention. He turned to see Noah standing before them with his hands full of ridiculously large books. Noah's wings opened wide and hummed. Arick's wings were humming as well, but he was unsure how to even begin to apologize.

"I—" Arick started.

Noah cleared his throat, stopping him. "The bat has come out of his cave," Noah teased and grinned.

His curly, brown hair hung around his hazel eyes, which

were filled with relief. Arick chuckled, feeling his wings relax in their natural position.

"I prefer to be called the almighty supreme heir instead," Arick replied sarcastically, earning another grin from Noah.

"This is why I don't babysit," Noah mumbled before shifting the books. "Is no one gonna help me with these ridiculous books?! Come on, ya lazy fairies."

Brock, Jared, and Galvin all scrambled to help lift the books out of Noah's arms.

"What are the books for?" Arick asked. He looked down at the books already on their table to inspect them. He was stunned as he read the covers.

History of Halflings: Memoirs of the Dead

Healing the Undead

Understanding the Demon World

"It is not much," Brock explained. "And the texts are so strange, they're hard to understand, but—" Brock trailed off.

"But we are trying," Noah finished. "We are trying to learn, to understand as much as we can."

Arick could feel despair and shame begin to consume him.

"I am a monster," Arick said softly. "There is nothing more to understand."

"But that is what is odd," Noah countered. "You are not exhibiting the 'normal' behaviors of other halflings in the past."

All Arick could do was stare at him. In his mind, this changed nothing. A monster was still a monster.

"What we've found so far is that, for some reason, you are different, Arick," Jared explained. "We are not sure why yet, but we are trying to find out through more research."

"Not only the behaviors either," Brock joined in. "Even your power and abilities are odd compared to the others in history."

Arick's wings flared in defense. No, he did not want to listen. Not even dare to hope for anything different for himself.

"We just need to do more digging and find out why," Jared continued.

"Enough," Arick commanded in a tone harsher than he intended. Silence followed. Arick cleared his throat to start again.

"I am sorry," Arick said roughly, ashamed at his outburst. "Besides, I have a mission I must complete." He looked at them. "I would like your help… please."

Brock, Jared, and Galvin all gave sideways glances at Noah. They soldiered under Raphael military, not the Michael. Noah looked between Arick and the others before rolling his eyes.

"Oh, fine." Noah sighed. "You can go with him."

They all released a breathe.

"I told you not to go stealing my soldiers," Noah grumbled to Arick.

Arick merely grinned. "I promise to return them."

Galvin caught Arick's eye and raised an eyebrow in question. Arick nodded to Galvin.

"Our mission is to go to the human realm and retrieve Atarah and Charlotte."

Brock and Jared's jaws dropped open, while Galvin appeared shocked. Unless one wanted to be a ranger, regular angels never visited the human realm. Noah's wings flared as his eyes turned sharp with focus.

"You're going to bring back Charlotte," Noah said, not as a question, but a statement.

Arick nodded all the same. He knew Noah had tried to stop the wedding, but by the time he sent out his messages, it had been too late. He guessed by Noah's twitching wings, he felt horrible about his family's plot. Arick didn't blame Noah nor have any anger toward him. In his mind, everything had been his fault. He bore the blame.

"We will bring them both back safe and sound," Arick

said. He patted Noah on the back. "It will be okay."

Noah sighed as his wings fell slightly.

"How can you or Charlotte forgive me?" Noah said softly.

"I believed you when you said you were on my side, Noah," Arick replied.

Noah's wings twitched once before slumping again. "I haven't always been on your side," he murmured.

"Well, you are now, and that's what matters," Arick replied. "In time, all wounds will be healed."

Noah exhaled slowly. "Tell Charlotte… I am sorry."

"Tell her yourself." Arick patted him once on the back, hard.

"Will you not join us, sir?" Brock asked Noah.

Noah shook his head. "No," he answered. "There is still much to be done in Azrael's region. My soldiers have helped with the female recovery for days now. It is one thing for me to come for a day to Quaesitor to gather information, but another thing entirely for me to go to the human realm."

Arick furrowed his brow. "Have none of you been in Mortem helping with the recovery?"

They shook their heads, but Noah answered.

"I've assigned them to do research. Research on halflings, demon psychology behavior, and past treatments."

Arick looked at all of them, baffled. Fondness mixed with hope filled Arick's chest. He tried to squash the feelings down, but to no avail. *No!* he thought. He was a monster, and nothing would change that.

"Go ahead and get ready for the journey," Arick commanded his team. "We meet at the Head Tree in an hour and head out from there."

"So soon?" Jared inquired.

Arick nodded. "My father said he's gathered enough power to transport us. From there, we will seek out Atarah and Charlotte and look for a ranger named Luke. He will help us get back."

"Luke?" Noah asked incredulously, drawing all of their attention.

"Yes, Luke," Arick replied tentatively.

Noah tucked his chin in and covered his mouth. His shoulders shook… with laughter, Arick realized.

"Good luck." Noah chuckled.

Arick groaned mentally. His father must have purposely skimped on some details. No matter. Arick was more than eager to go on the mission. Keen to get his hands on the serum to tame the power simmering within him. Arick turned toward his team, ignoring Noah's shaking, laughing form.

"Tonight," he commanded.

Tonight, they would enter the human realm with the chance to redeem his past failure. A chance to reconnect with his sister, whom he hadn't seen in weeks, almost months! Arick's wings flared and his muscles tensed. His power rose up within him, like water about to overflow. Arick clenched his fists together and willed his rage into submission. *Come on*, he prayed, *just hold off for a few more hours, and then it won't matter anymore.*

Chapter 4

Atarah glided across the buildings to keep up with the demon, while staying out of sight. *This demon is very selective,* Atarah thought. For the past few hours, the demon wandered around the town, scanning the faces of various humans to pick its next victim. The demon occasionally paused outside of a few restaurants and bars to smell the air with a contemplative look before continuing. It roamed the downtown street repeatedly, turning around and walking back down the same street.

While following the demon, Atarah was able to find out the name of the town. Whitefish, Montana. Not that it made much of a difference to Atarah. They were stranded here unless she could convince a ranger to send them back. She wondered what life was like for them in the human realm. Was it difficult to always drink the serum? She shuddered at the thought of her wings being trapped for so long.

The demon started to walk away from the downtown area, forcing them to switch to traveling on foot. Atarah didn't like it, but flying would attract attention. She jumped from the rooftop and landed softly. Close behind her were Charlotte and Ben, with Gabriel taking up the rear. They all tucked in their wings as tightly as possible before sprinting. They hid behind houses or trees, whatever they could, as they followed the demon. Atarah was grateful the night sky created its own black veil around them. She was certain they would've been spotted if it had been daylight.

They dove around trees and houses for several blocks until they crossed a bridge over a river. The demon walked further away from the town center. More and more trees surrounded them as they ventured toward a large park or nature preserve, Atarah suspected. The demon was here for a reason. Did it know they were following it? Or did it really have its sights set on a human?

"Ben," Atarah whispered. He appeared there instantaneously.

His face was covered in sweat, but his eyes were open and eager for her. He came in closer than Atarah anticipated. She felt the heat of his body up against her own. Her wings flared, while her heart fluttered.

"Yes?" Ben whispered back.

"Can you get a sense of what the demon is thinking?" Atarah whispered. She forced herself to relax, while Ben's wings hummed.

Ben nodded. His face looked passive, despite his humming wings. His brown hair fell over his eyes a little as he squinted them in concentration. He stayed silent for a moment before whispering close to her ear.

"It just keeps focusing on 'The Hunt,'" Ben spoke softly.

Atarah's wings vibrated on their own at the softness of his breath. She leaned into him involuntarily as he spoke.

"Its mind is not thinking of one thing in particular other than the thrill of the hunt," Ben continued.

"Do you hear any rangers close by?" Charlotte came up on Atarah's other side.

Ben shook his head. "It doesn't work like that. I wouldn't be able to discern if the person I heard was a ranger unless they specifically thought about it."

"What are we to do if that thing attacks a human?" Gabriel whispered loudly behind all of them. "Are we to just stand by, or are we going to attack and risk exposure?"

"I am not completely sure," Atarah answered honestly.

"We will be at a disadvantage, but I know I will want to do something to stop the demon from attacking."

Gabriel scoffed at her, but didn't stay anything further. Atarah could care less what Gabriel thought, but it was Charlotte who shot a glare at him. He took one glance at Charlotte and looked down sheepishly, as if ashamed. Atarah almost chuckled at their situation, but Ben drew her attention.

"Look!" he whispered. "It's turning into a park."

Atarah turned to see the demon disappear between the trees. She used her senses to make sure the coast was clear of any humans before signaling for them to move. They quickly ventured into the nature preserve, staying low to the ground. A weight lifted off her shoulders. Now they were away from the human residences. Nonetheless, her stomach tightened as the air shifted.

The air grew stale and the animals silent as they ventured further. A sinister energy expanded with each step they took. Eventually, they came to a large open field where the demon stood in the middle. The demon gazed up toward the starry sky with its back to them.

If we wanted to, we could ambush it, Atarah thought, but she paused.

She peered around the field, and something didn't sit well with her. As her gaze turned back to the demon before them, a sound emanated from the demon. At first, it sounded like a scratchy, gurgle sound, almost like a dry heave. The demon's body quivered and quaked with each sound it made. After a while, Atarah realized that the demon was laughing hysterically.

Ben's hand suddenly gripped her shoulder, squeezing painfully tight. Atarah bit her lip to keep any sound from escaping. Atarah turned her head to give him a questioning glance, but quickly saw that something was wrong. Ben's gorgeously tan face appeared abnormally pale. His eyes widened with fright, and his wings shook. Atarah expanded her power as far as she could to survey the surrounding area. There were no humans anywhere close to them, but a powerful threat was emerging.

Her heart raced as she sensed a familiar presence and a new one. From the aura that she picked up on, there were two terrifyingly powerful demons coming. Atarah watched with dread as a large, horrifying figure emerged from the darkness of the trees in front of the demon. Crawling forward with slowness and ease was an Abaddon.

Charlotte covered her mouth and ducked down further to the ground, her entire body shaking. Gabriel lowered himself also, shielding Charlotte with his body and wings. None of their gazes left the Abaddon. Ben and Atarah instinctively drew closer to one another, whether for courage or for strength, Atarah didn't know. For a brief moment, Atarah forgot all about what Ben, Gabriel, and Elizabeth had done to her. In that moment, all Atarah could think about was the pain inflicted upon her by the last Abaddon she had faced. Atarah's hands shook with fear, a kind of fear that was so consuming one could not move. She locked her eyes onto the scene in front of her, feeling petrified and helpless.

Another figure materialized through the shadows, smaller than the Abaddon, but still larger than most other angels. The figure had a broad chest, dark hair, and odd markings all over the arms and face. The figure drew closer to the single demon in the field, giving them a closer look.

The figure looked similar to her father.

However, Atarah knew immediately it was not her father. His dark, curly hair, golden eyes, strong jawline, and large stature were the same, but he bore no wings and his face looked more angular than her father's. A calculated coldness settled in his eyes that sent chills down her spine. He wore strange markings along the sides of his face and down his neck as if they had been burned into his skin. He appeared annoyed as he regarded the demon in front of him. He looked the demon up and down with little more than a sneer. The Abaddon growled viciously at the laughing demon. The demon stilled instantly and quieted. The demon bowed deeply before the figure, waiting for a command.

"Status report," the figure who looked similar to her father spoke.

His voice sounded deep and rich, but bored. His voice reminded her of Arick somehow. That must be the demon's leader. Did he have the ability to shape-shift? Why did it resemble her father?

The demon spoke in a language Atarah had never heard, nor did she want to hear it again. Atarah and her friends covered their ears. The language sounded like sharp, dry, high-pitched screeches with the occasional croaking or hissing sound. The sounds didn't faze or bother the Abaddon nor the imposter-looking man. The demon spoke for a few minutes before growing silent.

"Have you completed the task I had for you in the south?" the fake Mikael asked.

The demon dry heaved some more, as if answering. He gave a few nods as he listened, but his aura grew darker and darker as the demon screeched on. Suddenly, the demon before him began to screech, not in speech, but in pain. The demon's body crumbled to the ground, withering and slithering about, contorting its body in odd angles. Atarah felt the heaviness of his power from where they hid as he hardened the air around the field, crushing the demon. The imposter looked on as if tormenting demons was an everyday occurrence. After a few minutes, he released some of his hold.

"Oh?" the imposter said, as if amused. "What did you do wrong, you ask?" He grinned at the demon, a grin that made Atarah want to vomit. Though he bore a similar face to her father and brother, they were nothing like this monster.

"Nothing," the imposter said. "Well... mostly nothing."

He walked around the cowering demon with his hands

behind his back, as if he was taking a leisurely stroll.

"You did everything right up until the last moment," he continued. "For you see—" he stopped on the other side of the demon and stared off into the distance—"You let yourself be followed."

The imposter continued to look where they hid, beyond the field and behind the trees. All the blood in her body turned cold as his gaze landed on them. Her wings shook, but her body refused to move. She screamed inside her head, demanding her body to run, get to safety, but to no avail. Her body disconnected from her mind entirely.

The imposter lifted two fingers at Atarah and indicated for her to come forward. All on its own, her body stood and walked toward him, to her horror. Who—no, *what* was this creature before her? How was her body being controlled? Outwardly, she remained silent, but internally, she screamed for help. She fought hard to glance back at her companions, but saw all of them frozen with the same paralysis that consumed her. Only Ben's flickering eyes told her that he heard her pleas.

Tears fell down her face as she struggled to get out of this helpless situation. The closer she walked to him, the more glee he seemed to get from her dread and terror. She stopped just a few feet in front of him, completely paralyzed. He surveyed her up and down in a way that made her skin crawl. A vile grin spread onto his face as he regarded her.

"You look a lot like someone I know, little angel," his voice purred. "I think I'll keep this one." He directed his voice to the Abaddon. "But the rest of those—" he waved a hand at where her friends were—"feel free to have as much fun as you want with them."

"No," a small, strangled whisper escaped her lips.

His grin only widened. He started to raise his hand toward her face when a violent blast struck down in front of Atarah and resonated like thunder. She felt the power deep in her chest as she was knocked several feet back. Those precious few seconds were enough for Atarah to break free from her paralysis and bolt to her friends. They all shook free from their own paralysis and stood onto their feet.

"FLY UP! FLY!" Atarah screamed.

None of them hesitated. They all shot into the sky like rockets. She lifted into the sky as fast as she could, to escape the ground.

Howls and shrieks erupted from behind Atarah, but she didn't dare look back. She flew as fast as she could, as high as she could, to get away. They all flew like angels out of hell, out of the park, not paying attention to where they were going.

After a moment, Atarah noticed they had flown out of the town and were headed for the hills they had arrived on. Back to where they started. Charlotte was the first one to land back on the hill, followed by Gabriel, and then Ben. Atarah lowered her feet to land when a heavy force slammed into her, causing her to crash-land on the hill. Ben was immediately by her side, his wings flared, body lowered in a defense position. Atarah jumped to her feet to see what slammed into her.

A large angel landed with a force that shook the hill they stood on. Atarah refused to let her fear show. She flared her wings wider and moved into her fighting stance. Gabriel stood protectively in front of Charlotte with his wings expanded. In the darkness, Atarah made out a smaller figure landing gently beside the large angel, but she could not see any details yet from either of them.

"Who are you?" Atarah said with a harsh tone. Adrenaline pumped through her as she feared being followed by the demons.

A spark ignited into a small flame in front of the smaller angel, giving Atarah a better view. Atarah's wings slumped in relief. The flame revealed two rangers. A large female angel and a short male angel, who carried the flame. The female was large with ebony skin and dark hair in a single, tight braid.

With her stature and built muscles, Atarah immediately knew she was from the Michael Clan. She wore dark cargo pants, a long sleeve top, and combat boots.

Atarah glanced at the male angel. He possessed bright red hair and rectangular glasses that sat on his face. Though his face appeared young, she guessed from how he carried himself that he was older. His brown eyes looked between the three of them in a curious, thoughtful way.

He must be from the Uriel Clan, Atarah thought.

He also wore dark clothing that covered almost all of his body, with combat boots. This must be the rangers' uniform.

"Easy there, kids." The male's voice was soothing.

Not that it helped Atarah. Atarah was still frazzled by the demon encounter and didn't want to let her guard down yet.

"Easy there. You are safe now. The demons have fled back to their world now. No harm will come to you." The male raised his other hand, as if to say he was harmless. "My name is Flynn, and this is my partner, Imani."

Flynn waved his hand toward Imani as a way of introduction. Imani looked all of them up and down with vague disgust. Her face was unimpressed.

Atarah glanced between them and slowly turned her head toward Ben to her left.

Are they safe? she thought.

Ben heard her question and gave a tiny nod. Neither meant any harm. Once Atarah relaxed her wings, everyone else followed suit.

"My name is Atarah," she said firmly.

Imani's wings twitched, while her eyes widened. Flynn didn't catch on to his partner's reaction as he regarded all of them with equal curiosity.

"To my left is Ben, and behind me are Charlotte and Gabriel," Atarah introduced them.

Both of them jumped that time. No other angels had that name, except the heir and the Head Arch. The smallest shift in their faces took place. Flynn no longer appeared curious, but mildly irritated, while Imani outright sneered.

"Worse than a bunch of spaceheads, Flynn." Imani scoffed. "We have some royal spaceheads."

"It would seem so." Flynn's eyes sharpened on them, calculating.

"All we want is passage back to the Spirit realm," Charlotte spoke up softly from behind Atarah.

Flynn and Imani looked incredulously at her before tipping their heads back and laughing. Big, boisterous laughs that shook their shoulders.

"You hear this, Flynn?" Imani said between chuckles.

"Oh yeah," Flynn said with sarcasm. "This little princess has the audacity to ask for a ride through the realms, while *standing* right next to *Gabriel*." Flynn's lip curled in irritation at his name.

Gabriel shifted his weight over to block Charlotte from their jeers. His wings wrapped around her protectively.

"Aw, look at this," Imani said mockingly. "The little prince even has a crush on her!"

Flynn and Imani laughed callously, while Gabriel blushed bright red.

"Sometimes it surprises me how spoiled you spaceheads can get, up in your world," Flynn taunted.

She forced herself to remain calm, despite the growing irritation within her. She wouldn't have cared if they had continued to make fun of her, but Charlotte was a different story. Her adrenaline rush had stopped, which was helping her think more clearly. They had found two rangers; now she needed to act before they were stranded… again.

"It surprises me how little informed you both are," Atarah said softly.

Flynn looked tempted to roll his eyes, while Imani glared at her.

"You'd be surprised by how much we know, so watch

your tongue, princess," Imani hissed back.

Atarah remained cool. *Still a diplomat*, she reminded herself. She had to bridge gaps. If she lost her composure now, she would be a failure.

"Then with your immense knowledge," Atarah said, taking a step closer to them. "Do either of you have any idea how odd it is that you've found, not just one or two, but *four* Arch heirs within a relatively short distance from two incredibly powerful demons?"

Flynn and Imani grew somber. She was right. No matter how much they ridiculed them, the situation was severe.

"Why don't you help us put all the pieces together then?" Flynn asked smoothly.

Ben shook his head. "Not so fast there," Ben said, raising his finger at them.

Flynn and Imani's wings flared. Atarah bit her lip to keep from laughing. Ben purposely baited them.

"You have the audacity to ask us for help after mocking us?" Ben used their words against them. "My, my, how spoiled you earth dwellers have become."

Flynn rolled his eyes this time, exasperated, while Imani looked furious beside him.

"Well played, prince," Flynn said acerbically. "Come with us and we can find someone in our pod to help *after* you give us all the information you have on that Luciferian and the Abaddon."

Luciferian! Atarah felt like she was hit with a ton of bricks. She had learned and read about Luciferians as legend, a thing of the past. A monster so horrendous, it took the power of two Arch Heads to defeat one.

Ben gripped her arm to keep her steady on her feet. Atarah couldn't keep the shock off her face if she tried. She leaned toward Ben for support. His wings hummed.

"Ugh, great!" Imani sighed. "Looks like we got a couple of lovers on our hands."

"It's complicated," Atarah and Charlotte said in unison.

Atarah scrambled away from Ben. They glanced at each other, while Flynn and Imani scoffed.

"All right, we can't sit here all night, kids," Flynn spoke up. "We will fly to HQ and there Luke will want to do a debrief with each of you."

Flynn extinguished the flame in his hand and opened his wings wide. Imani mimicked him.

"Try to keep up," Imani taunted before they shot up into the air.

I guess that is as much information as we will get, Atarah thought. She worried what they would tell them once they got to 'HQ.'

"Don't worry," Ben whispered to her. "I got a small glimpse into what the Luciferian had in mind for the human realm and our realm. We can use that to our advantage."

"Oh, *we*?" Atarah said, raising her eyebrow. She took another step away from him. "Don't think that this changes anything between us."

Ben winced. "Please, Atarah," he whispered fervently. "Give me a chance. You can't hide the truth from me. I know you're hurt, but I also know your true feelings for me. I know you care for me just as much as I do for you."

"I guess you're going to have to earn that chance," Atarah replied coldly. She didn't like her feelings for him being used against her. "*Properly* this time."

Ben flinched at the memory of his promise back in her home mountains.

"We are not going to wait on you all night," Imani yelled from above.

Atarah launched herself into the air. Charlotte followed close behind her and then the guys lifted up last. All of them flew off into the dark, starry night with no clue as to where they were heading.

Elijah walked out of his office, exhausted after a long day of reading and writing reports. The latest report came from Mikael. Elijah hadn't heard from him since the Lanua incident, but Elijah had sent a numerous number of letters since then. After receiving the urgent note from Noah, revealing the full truth to Elijah about Mikael and Arick, Elijah flew as fast as he could to Urbs Antiqua. Upon arrival, Elijah saw the aftermath of Arick's rage from the monster within him. He quickly found his wife, thoroughly shaken, and connected what had happened from Gabriel Sr. and his guards. Arick had shown his true colors as a demon and attacked everyone before departing. He, along with his team, reported back to Mikael, which urged Elijah into action. When Noah sent his letter explaining what Arick truly was, his stomach dropped. How could Mikael allow such a thing to happen? He couldn't believe Elizabeth and Charlotte had been so close to such a monster! While he hadn't liked his wife's plan to marry Charlotte off, he felt relief when she was away from everything dangerous.

After days of waiting, Elijah received a report from Mikael. He reported that he sent Arick and his team to the human realm to retrieve Atarah *and* Charlotte. He explained that Charlotte would be returned to them safely and unmarried. Mikael asked for peace between houses for the sake of his wife and children. He gave a veiled threat that if anything else were to happen, he wouldn't hold back his own anger.

However, Elijah barely registered the threat. Arick was being sent to bring back the girls? How could Mikael trust him? Could he trust Arick after everything that was revealed? He needed to share the news with Elizabeth.

Elijah cautiously knocked on the bedroom door, as to not alarm his wife. He peeked in to check on her, surprised to find her balled up in an uneasy sleep. Since he had retrieved Elizabeth from Lanua, she had come down with a strange sickness that none of their healers, nor even him, could pinpoint. There was nothing *physically* wrong, but he knew Elizabeth wasn't well. For days, she stayed up at night, fearful of Arick or Mikael's revenge against her. She had become so fearful and riddled with anxiety, her appetite had disappeared. His beautiful wife lost an unusual amount of weight in only a few days since their failed plot.

Her lack of sleep and weight loss had taken such a toll that Elijah feared for her. She screamed or attacked anyone she did not trust, which was virtually everyone but Elijah. He entered quietly, so he wouldn't wake her. He walked to the side of the bed and gazed down at his wife with worry. Her face tensed as he moved closer. She tossed and turned in discomfort. He debated waking her when her journal caught his eye.

Her trusted journal, a true window into what went on inside her mind. He had always respected her privacy, but now his concern for her overrode her confidentiality. He grabbed her journal and settled into a chair close by the bed, so he could stay by her side.

The journal was large and thick, filled with Elizabeth's words. The diary had been made and bound out of oak wood, which gave it a hard exterior. He unclasped the latch and flipped through the pages. He admired her neat and elegant handwriting for a moment before noticing a shift in writing style.

For most of the journal, her handwriting was normal and fluid; however, as Elijah turned the pages toward the more recent entries, he noticed a difference. Her handwriting turned more scratchy, hard, and sloppy. Elijah squinted his eyes, confused. Surely, this could not be his wife's handwriting? It looked as if someone else wrote in her journal. Elijah turned to her last entry and read.

They can't be trusted... No one can be trusted. What am I to do? What left is there to do other than... No! No! That idea is a last resort. I must remember this is to bring my family together…

"What are you doing?"

Elijah jumped. Elizabeth sat up in their bed, her disheveled hair sticking up in every direction, her eyes sunken. Her green nightgown hung loosely around her shoulders. She stared at her journal in his hand, and her gaze turned hard and suspicious. Elijah closed the journal and gently set it aside before crouching down to kneel before her beside the bed.

"I didn't want to wake you, my dear." Elijah grabbed hold of her hand. Her hand felt like an icicle.

"You are so cold, my love. Here, let me warm you." Elijah rubbed his hands around her own in an effort to generate heat. "I will get some more blankets for you."

"Elijah."

"Yes, dear?"

"Why were you reading my journal?" Her voice sounded detached and apathetic. Her eyes glued to her journal. Her gaze appeared as cold as her hand.

"I wanted to know what you were thinking," Elijah explained. "I am worried about you, my dear."

"Hmmm," Elizabeth said. Her face remained impassive.

"Are you hungry?" Elijah asked, concerned by her demeanor.

Elizabeth didn't say anything, just continued to stare at the journal. Her wings slumped as a single tear fell from her face. Elijah quickly wiped it away. He pondered what more he could do for her. Nothing came to mind.

A soft knock on the door drew Elijah's attention, while Elizabeth's wings flared. She drew back her top lip as if she was about to hiss, but no sound came out. Elijah fastened his grip on her hands as a way to calm her.

"Hold on a minute," Elijah shouted.

Elijah rose from the side of the bed gently to not disturb his wife. He opened the door slightly, enough for his torso, and that was all. Outside the door stood one of their long-standing servants of the house, Kinsley. He stood small in stature, so Elijah didn't see him at first. Elijah always liked Kinsley for his witty humor and his speed.

"A message for you, sir," Kinsley said, holding out a small scroll wrapped up in twine. "It came from one of Noah's soldiers in Mortem."

"Thank you, Kinsley." Elijah took the small scroll. "Make sure no one else disturbs this room tonight, all right?"

"Yes, sir." With that, Kinsley bounded off.

Elijah closed the door gently before turning to Elizabeth with a smile.

"Did you hear that? We have news from Noah!" Elijah exclaimed, hoping the news would excite his wife.

"Noah?" Elizabeth said distantly. Her wings slumped back onto the bed, and her eyes turned unfocused. Elijah hurriedly joined her back at her side and opened the scroll.

"It says, 'Dear Father, I will keep this report short, for I have some good news. The brigade and I will return home to Silva in the next few days. Due to the lack of demon activity, along with the safe return of the females to the Vallis region, our aid is no longer needed. My soldiers are excited to return home. I am also excited because I have much to share with you from the knowledge I've gained from the Library of Quaesitor. Sewall sends his gratitude, and I hope to see both of you soon. With love, your son, Noah.' This is amazing news, my dear!"

Elijah glanced to Elizabeth's face to see if there was any sort of relief or joy, but saw none. She didn't appear to be listening to him. Elijah grew more worried. He grabbed both of her hands once more and brought them to his lips. Despair spread through him as he thought fruitlessly of what to do for her. He lowered her hand and gently pushed her back onto the bed.

"Please rest, my dear," Elijah coaxed.

She went down with no fight. Just with sunken, unfocused eyes and a pale look on her face that disturbed him. He looked at Noah's words on the note and wondered what could help.

Most of his major healers remained scattered throughout the Spirit realm. He could call one back, but winced at taking away aid when many regions were filled with injured soldiers. He thought about his son and then stiffened as he thought of a possible solution.

Charlotte. Charlotte was one of the few major healers who could be on her way back from the human realm. *Surely, Charlotte would look at her mother and be able to heal her?* Elijah wondered. Elijah thought about the possibilities. *Will Charlotte even see her mother or will she be too angry at them for her rushed wedding ceremony?*

Elijah shook his head. With Noah and Charlotte coming home, maybe that would help lift Elizabeth's spirit. What other options did he have? Elijah leaned down and kissed her forehead.

"I will be right back, my dear," Elijah whispered. "I am just going to the library real quick."

Elizabeth stared up at the wall, almost lifeless. Elijah's heart clenched at the sight of her. Elizabeth was vibrant, gentle, and kind. Not this dull form before him, nor someone riddled with anger or anxiety. After pulling the covers over her with care, he made his way down to their private library. The library wasn't the usual kind with books held in a straight and linear angle. Their library had books lined the way the branches moved in their home tree. The branches bent in every direction, which gave the library a chaotic look. The books were sometimes stacked vertically, others horizontally.

Tonight, the library laid empty and dark. Elijah lit several lanterns and started his research. He started with an array of books:

Study of the Mind, Emotions, and Spirit
Power of the Mind

Healing Inside and Out
Restoring the Soul
Rehabilitate the Spirit

Just a few to start with, he thought. He would be damned if he, the Archangel Head of the Raphael Clan, could do nothing for his very own wife! He read through the pages with speed and expertise. *Please hold on my dear,* Elijah prayed. He would work all night if he had to, if it meant getting his wife back.

Arick landed softly onto the ground with ease, while his team landed unceremoniously behind him. Except for Galvin, who looked at Jared and Brock's landing with mild amusement. Arick grimaced at the small vials in his hand. The bitter liquid known as the serum suppressed their wings and powers to blend into the human realm. Arick loathed the taste, but for once, he was eager to have his powers suppressed. Arick quickly drank the serum in a single shot and gagged at the bitter aftertaste.

"Okay, on with it," Arick said, handing the serum to Brock, Jared, and Galvin. As they grabbed their vials, Arick's wings quivered while the serum took effect.

Each angel looked apprehensive. This was their first time tasting the serum. Brock was the first one brave enough to drink. His downfall was that he took a small sip instead of a huge gulp and began to heave.

"Don't be a scared fairy," Jared said with bravo, and attempted to gulp down his serum.

Jared's face screwed with disgust and he started to gag as well. Arick tried to hide the amusement on his face, but failed miserably. Brock chugged most of his portion. Both of their faces resembled a baby trying a lemon for the first time. Arick coughed to hide his chuckle before giving Galvin the last vial.

"Bottoms up," Arick said.

Galvin grabbed the bottle—no hesitation—and gulped it down. Brock, Jared, and Arick all waited for his reaction. Galvin looked down at the bottle and back at them before shrugging. No revulsion, disgust, or effect.

"Arghhhhhhh!" Brock groaned as Jared finished the serum.

"You're lying, Vin," Jared grumbled. "This is the grossest thing I've ever had."

Galvin held his hands up further in a shrug.

Arick and Jared shuddered as the serum worked. The process was quite painless as the wings shrunk and folded in on themselves. Soon enough, the wings absorbed into their backs with a dull ache that would grow over time. Restraints around their powers tightened, like a constricting jacket.

Arick stood wingless and powerless. Jared and Galvin marveled at their bare backs for a moment, while Arick surveyed their surroundings. It was nighttime, but that mattered little for the bright city. His father said the current Headquarters for the Rangers was located in a place called New York City. He described a city that 'never sleeps' for demons, and angels never rested.

Arick and his team hid in a back alleyway, a place his father called Harlem. Arick thought back on his father's instructions.

"You need to get to Central Park and find the location called the ramble. That is where you can signal the rangers to let you into their headquarters," Mikael explained.

He had assembled them before the burgundy Head Tree in Quaesitor. Arick took out his more human clothes, which were his black cargo pants and a plain, gray shirt. He had told his team to wear clothes that did not have any symbols. Nothing that would stick out, like their soldier uniform or insignia bearing jacket. Mikael inspected their outfits before handing Arick the four vials of serum.

"You can get more once you find the headquarters. They

have their own… variation of the serum."

"Are they not the same?" Arick inquired.

Mikael grimaced. "No," he explained. "There are three different kinds of the serum. Our serum was created for very short-term use, only a few hours. The other two serums are meant for long-term use by the rangers. One lasts for 3-4 months and the last one—the longest acting serum—lasts for a full year. I would caution you when taking their serum. With the long-lasting serum, you can control when your wings are hidden, but it is very, very painful. So, most rangers do not like to bring their wings out unless absolutely necessary." Mikael winced. "Most rangers take the yearly dose, but they should have the 3-4 month version too."

"But with the long-lasting serum, we won't be stuck in human form. We'll still be able to use our powers. Just hide our wings," Arick said more as a statement than a question.

"That is correct. The rangers have never been a fan of our way of life in the Spirit realm. They are considered outcasts in our world, but in the human realm, they are at home." He paused as he studied Arick. "Don't be stupid when interacting with them," Mikael said sincerely.

Arick's wings had flared. That was his father's version of 'please be careful,' but why did he always have to sound like a jackass?

Mikael took a step back. His hands vibrated and glowed, whether from his power or from the force he exerted, Arick wasn't sure. Heat radiated from his father. The portal fascinated him each time his father opened the divide between realms. Mikael brought his hands together and began to pull apart an invisible seam. Mikael strained and flexed all the muscles in his hands as he created an opening. His father grunted with effort. Sweat dripped down his brow after a few moments. Arick started to worry that his father hadn't built up enough power to create the opening.

He had been wrong. Slowly, a thin, white line appeared

before them. It started off thin and then grew thicker and thicker with Mikael's effort. Soon, a tall, blazing oval opened. Almost as tall as the Head Tree, the portal emanated heat and pure energy that gave him goosebumps. The thrum of power always sent a healthy amount of fear through Arick. Mikael breathed with effort to keep the portal open.

"Go." A single harsh word from Mikael.

Arick took a running jump into the portal, quickly followed by his team. Going through the realms created a sensation of weightlessness and heavy flight. The rush of falling, but the heaviness of his body prevented him from thrashing around. His wings opened reflexively only to be stopped by some unknown magnetic force as he fell through the portal. Colors, lights, and time whirled around them in incoherent patterns, disorienting Arick for a moment before everything became still. Like spinning round and round, with flashing lights and suddenly coming to a stop. The next moment, Arick had landed in the human realm, trying to figure out where they needed to go next.

Arick brought himself out of the memory and into the present. No human had seen their arrival or transformation, which was always the first thing. Now, all they needed to do was head south and follow the signs for Central Park. Once in Central Park, they needed to get to the ramble and somehow signal the rangers. Arick hadn't a single clue of how to do that other than have their wings out.

I guess we'll figure it out along the way, he thought.

"I've never felt so light in my entire life!" Jared exclaimed behind him.

Jared turned his head in wonder at his wingless back. Galvin twirled around in excitement next to him. He appeared marveled by how fast he could turn around without his wings. It was easier to see behind you when wings weren't in the way.

Arick noticed Brock hadn't finished his vial and still had

his wings out.

"Brock!" Arick whispered. "Quickly drink the rest before we are seen!"

"Ugghhhh," Brock responded weakly. He looked slightly green.

"Here." Jared came up behind him and took the vial. "Just chug it down. Don't even think about it!"

He tilted Brock's head back and dumped the contents of the vial down his throat. Brock sputtered and choked as the serum made its way down. Brock pushed Jared away as he gagged on the serum in his throat. He coughed so loudly that Arick worried about drawing attention.

"SHUT UP!" someone yelled nearby, their voice thick with an accent Arick couldn't place.

Arick sighed in relief as Brock's wings shrank and folded in on themselves. Finally, Brock stood, completely fine and also amazed.

"Woah!" Brock exclaimed. "Do humans always see *everything* behind them?" He began turning his head dramatically. "I feel like an owl! I can see everything behind me."

Jared and Galvin shared a laugh, while Arick grinned himself.

"Alright, fairies," Arick drew their attention. "Now that we are socially acceptable, we gotta move." He turned around and pointed toward the street. "Our destination is a place called the ramble in Central Park. It is a popular destination, so we should have no problem finding it. Any questions?" Arick meant for the last part to be rhetorical, but his team asked him questions anyway.

"Will we get to try some human food, oh great drama queen?" Brock gave a dramatic bow.

"I wanna go to the tops of these buildings!" Jared shouted.

Galvin turned his head every which way, looking at the lights of the city, his eyes too wide with excitement to focus.

Arick groaned at them. "This is why I shouldn't babysit,"

he grumbled.

"What was that?" Jared and Brock looked at him, amused.

"Never mind," Arick said, shaking his head. "First, the ramble, then,"—Arick held up a finger, drawing their attention once more—"we get pizza and ice cream."

Brock, Jared, and Galvin all roared in excitement.

"HEY! SHUT UP DOWN THERE!" the same person yelled as before.

They all laughed as they walked toward the street.

Once on the street, Arick felt like he was herding cats, constantly grabbing Brock by the collar to drag him away from the food stands, while Jared attempted to leap into the air to get to the tops of buildings. Galvin was the only one who stood close by, but he often spaced out in wonder, gazing at the city, slowing them down. Arick dragged him around too. Every time he looked over his shoulder to make sure they were following him, he'd find them spread out. Most humans didn't even glance at them. Maybe an occasional annoyed glance or a scoffed 'ugh, tourist' comment, but other than that, they were left alone.

It was not hard to find Central Park. They quickly found signs for Central Park, leading away from the busier streets. At night, the city was quieter than Arick expected. Several humans with bulky clothing and disheveled looks wandered about with a few rats at the entrance.

All right, almost there, Arick thought with relief.

Away from the city streets, Brock, Jared, and Galvin came back to focus, though the excitement had not yet worn off.

The trees, in the distance, gave Arick a sense of familiarity and peace, while the concrete roads filled with trash made him balk. Arick found little excitement and wonder in the city because he saw it as disgusting with too many people. He had been to the human realm before, so this city didn't overwhelm him.

"Hey," Arick whispered to his team. Without his wings,

he couldn't signal them like he normally would, so he'd have to use words. "Keep your guard up. Demons like to roam around here too."

That did the trick.

Brock, Jared, and Galvin straightened their backs and sharpened their gazes, alert and watching. He knew some demons made it their life's mission to find the ranger's headquarters, but they failed. Arick wondered why. How would they be able to find it and not the demons? Also, how long would the headquarters be there? So many questions entered Arick's mind now that they were here.

While they walked along Fifth Avenue, Arick stayed alert, but went into his thoughts once more. When they were in the headquarters, could they find this Luke ranger his father spoke about? What was Luke like exactly? Also, why did he need him to find Atarah and Charlotte? Arick's chest burned with anger when he remembered that his sister was not alone. Ben and Gabriel Jr. were with them. He doubted either of them could hurt Atarah physically, but she had been betrayed. Arick shook his head in disgust. He had liked Ben too! He had thought of him trustworthy until he tried to force Atarah into a marriage for his own political gain. As for Gabriel… Arick didn't think much of him for he knew very little. He knew his father and Gabriel Sr. had a complicated relationship, an allyship his father once described, but now Arick wasn't sure.

He had seen Gabriel Jr. only a handful of times growing up. Gabriel had always looked like a shy, stuttering nerd to Arick. He barely paid him a second glance. Well, now Gabriel Jr. had caught his full attention. He knew his father wanted peace, so he wouldn't start anything with Ben or Gabriel, but… Arick tightened his jaw. He would make sure they knew the trust was gone.

They came upon a large, roman renaissance style building that stretched on for several streets. The signs said the Metropolitan Museum of Art, but all Arick focused on was that they were close to the ramble. Arick quickened his steps and his squad followed closely. Eager to get some answers, he turned off of Fifth Avenue and dove into Central Park. The trees surrounded them quickly, which gave Arick mild comfort. His heart raced as they travelled deeper into the park. The hairs on the back of his neck stood up. An urgency began to take place in his chest that he couldn't explain. So close to completing his mission, to not being a failure. He picked up the pace. In less than an hour, he made it to what he thought was the ramble.

He moved through the bushes and the trees, paying attention to details that could give them clues. Without his powers to enhance his senses, he was fairly vulnerable. Exposed. He looked around for a sign of rangers, but just found trees, bushes, and trash.

"Fan out and look for any signs," Arick whispered to Brock, Jared, and Galvin.

They all spread out and moved quietly past tree branches. Arick was grateful for the trees and nighttime coverage. The hairs on the back of his neck continued to tingle as he searched. It was as if someone was watching them.

"Are you lost?" a voice called out behind Arick.

He whirled around to see a burly man. He wore layers of dirty clothing, though it was mid-summer in the human realm. His hat covered most of his scraggly hair that fell around his chin, and his beard appeared unkempt with food crumbs all around. He was of average human height with deep brown eyes. At least, that was as much as Arick could discern of him in the night.

"No," Arick answered. "I am just searching."

"Ah," the homeless man said. "Be careful what you look for around these parts."

Arick half-turned to keep peering into the bushes and grass to search more, but something in Arick urged him to keep talking to the man.

"I said I am searching," Arick continued. "Not looking."

The man turned back to Arick with an odd look. "Oh?" He squinted his eyes at Arick. He sounded excited by what Arick had said. "What do you mean?"

"Looking implies I know what to see when I've found it," Arick explained. "Searching... Well, I don't know what I will see, but I will understand once I've found it."

The man regarded Arick pensively. "You are searching for something that you don't know or understand?" the man asked in an excited tone.

"I suppose I am," Arick said distantly. He continued to push and pull the bushes to and fro.

"I think I understand what you are searching for then," the man said quietly.

Arick turned around and surveyed the man once more. The man stood a little taller with a sharp, new look in his eyes. Arick had thought his eyes were a deep brown, but now his eyes shined with a golden-brown color. His unhinged appearance became honed for a split second.

Arick straightened up. "Luke?"

The man smiled. "It is nice to meet a fellow seeker."

Arick stiffened with disbelief. *They found him! That was fast!*

"Come. Gather your men and follow me," Luke whispered.

"Brock! Galvin! Jared!" Arick shouted.

All three heard him and popped their heads out from the bushes in opposite directions. They quickly walked to Arick, who moved closer to Luke with amazement. He had actually found him. Finding Luke within the first few hours of being in the human realm was incredible. He expected it to take days before he could find a ranger to lead them to headquarters.

"Where is the Headquarters? Is there a barrier hiding it?" Arick asked, looking around. The building must be massive with floors full of maps, information, or technology. He wondered how they kept such a large operation hidden from the demons.

"This way," Luke said quietly.

They followed him through the ramble cautiously. The amount of ragged clothing made it easy to keep an eye on Luke as they moved. They stalked through the brush to arrive in a clearing of sorts. More of a makeshift homeless camp. Dozens of hunched over figures all regarded them as they came into the clearing.

Arick paused in confusion for two reasons. One, he'd thought they were going to the headquarters, but they were in the open space of the park, forming a shabby circle. Two, he saw his sister Atarah, a part of the group, directly across from him. Atarah didn't see him at first. She looked deep in thought and her wings were flared. She appeared healthy and whole. Last time he had seen her, her eyes were drawn, her face pale, and her body weakened and trembling from exhaustion. Charlotte, who had been standing right by Atarah, noticed him across the opening and nudged Atarah. She glanced up to Arick and gasped. Her eyes widened in disbelief and her wings hummed.

Arick released the tension around his shoulders. He hadn't realized how anxious he had been. He took a step toward his sister. One step was all he took before Atarah sprinted forward and practically body slammed him into a massive hug. Arick wrapped his arms around her small frame and gave a gentle squeeze. Tension he had never noticed in his back, face, and neck loosened. Finally, he had made it through the human world to find Luke and bring his sister back. For this one time, he had not been the epic failure everyone expected.

Charlotte stood off to the side awkwardly until Arick waved her forward. Charlotte looked different than the last time he had seen her. Her cheekbones sharpened and held hurt in her eyes that she hadn't carried before. Pity swelled in his chest for Charlotte. She was stuck in the middle of all of their situations.

"Hey, cricket," Arick said softly in greeting.

Atarah gave a muffled response against his clothing. Arick chuckled before giving Charlotte a polite nod and smile.

"Hello, Charlotte," Arick spoke.

Charlotte blushed, but didn't look away this time. "H-hello, Arick," Charlotte stammered.

At this point, Brock, Jared, and Galvin all gathered around him, staring at Atarah and Charlotte in slight amazement. Galvin, in particular, seemed to have his eyes glued to Charlotte, who blushed even more.

"Arick never told us his sisters were hot," Jared whispered to Brock, who elbowed him.

"The one turning beet red is my aunt," Arick said as he rolled his eyes.

Atarah backed away from Arick and regarded his men. Arick resisted the urge to smile as his men squirmed under her scrutiny.

Brock coughed lightly and gave a small bow. "Brock Ezuil at your service, heir," he said softly.

Arick froze with bewilderment. He had never heard Brock's last name before. He'd never thought to ask. Jared and Galvin gave similar bows.

"I am Jared Wheuit, and this is Galvin Ariquel at your service. We are with the Raphael army, but our commander Noah allowed us on this mission."

"Please stand up," Atarah said stiffly.

She glanced at the others around them. Many stared with disgust plain on their faces. The rest of the rangers surrounded them, Arick noted.

"Looks like more spaceheads have come down through the realms to join our little princess," a voice shouted in front of Arick. A small ginger-haired man stepped forward with a large, stockier female behind him.

Atarah sighed. "Flynn's favorite pastime is to come up

with clever nicknames for us."

The one Atarah named Flynn approached, along with a few others. If Arick had his wings out, he would have flared them reactively. Brock, Jared, and Galvin all widened their stances, getting in a defensive position. Flynn and the huddled group around him sneered at them in distaste.

"Woah! Hold on now!" Luke called out.

He jumped in between them. Dropping the hulking blanket that had been on his back, his wings now spread in between them. Arick's eyes widened at the sight of the ebony, dragon-like wings. Luke was from the Michael Clan.

"Flynn, Flynn, Flynn," Luke chided. "I know our new arrivals seem like a troublesome burden, but it is actually good they are here. You just have yet to see it." Luke turned to Atarah. "Atarah." He leaned in closer toward her face. "I have a good feeling about this. Serendipity, Atarah. Serendipity."

Atarah quirked her head to the side.

"Feels like we are speaking the same language and yet have completely different understanding," Arick spoke.

Luke looked at him with wide eyes and an elated expression. "Exactly! Yes! Exactly, Arick!" Luke patted his hand roughly on Arick's back.

"Luke?" a familiar voice said to their left.

Arick turned to see Ben and Gabriel Jr. standing hesitantly to the side of them. Arick's muscles tensed up and his jaw tightened. Those two, he thought with animosity, were responsible for everything. Arick took a step toward them, but stopped short as Luke stepped in between them. Luke had his back to Arick, facing Ben.

"You are looking for clarity in a lot of ways," Luke answered Ben, who spoke earlier.

A puzzled expression came across Ben's face as Luke approached. Ben's brow furrowed in confusion as he listened to Luke's thoughts.

"You are not—" Ben's voice faded away as if his focus

was being pulled.

"Are? What a limiting word, yet full of possibilities," Luke mused. He frowned as if the word offended him.

"*These* are the rangers?" Gabriel Jr. asked in disbelief at the surrounding huddle of homeless people. "And *this* is their leader?"

All the rangers' wings flared in reaction to Gabriel's disdainful tone. When the wings flared, the cluster of clothing and blankets fell away from their bodies, revealing wings of all shapes, sizes, and colors. Many of the feathers glistened in the moonlight that came through the branches above.

"Yes," Flynn said softly, with a frosty bite. "This is our leader Luke, the—"

"Eccentric," Arick finished. His father's words echoed in his mind. Arick realized the true meaning behind what his father had told him. Nothing about the rangers was normal. They were different. Quirky. Outcasts, like he said.

"Quite suitable," Luke murmured, taking off his hat and shaking out his hair.

With the moonlight shining in the open space, Arick realized Luke's hair was dark purple. In this light, Arick could see his face better. What he saw surprised him. Luke stood tall and possessed a stocky frame like Michael angels, but his eyes and hair told a different lineage. His eyes had a golden ring along the outer edge of the iris that faded to black as it closed around the pupil. His round face had a full, purple beard, announcing his mixed heritage. Arick had never seen someone with his coloring before.

"Now, now, now, now, now, now," Luke walked around, glancing in different directions. "A conference is in order. No! A symposium is required," Luke announced, coming to a stop beside the short angel with glasses.

"My dear Flynn." Luke patted Flynn's shoulder. "Please indulge me with what events took place around you."

Flynn and the others stood in a formation with arms behind their backs, heads held high in salute, while Luke spoke. Despite their disheveled appearances, they were well-trained soldiers who held Luke in high regard.

"Sir, Imani and I were en route to investigate a disturbance that occurred around 48 N and 114W. An unusual spot for a demon to choose."

The large female Arick saw before spoke up. "Upon arrival, we saw these four"—she nodded toward Ben, Gabriel, Atarah, and Charlotte—"following a messenger demon, which led them to an Abaddon and another powerful demon." Her face curled into a sneer. "Of course, they did not hide themselves properly, so the unknown entity almost overtook them. Flynn and I intervened by throwing a surprise combination attack, offering them enough of a distraction to escape."

"Properly hide ourselves?" Gabriel said incredulously. "We did the best we could!"

"Silence, spacehead," Flynn hissed.

Their faces all remained expressionless, including the person Arick presumed to be Imani. Her tall athletic stature, ebony skin, strong jaw, and long locs of hair made her an intimidating figure. Arick was surprised he hadn't noticed her more. Luke paced around randomly in the small clearing as he took in the information. His brows furrowed in concentration.

"Afterward"—Imani continued as if no one had interrupted—"we followed them back to some small hilltops where we found out their true origin. A couple of spacehead, royal lovers trapped in the human realm."

"We led them back here for questioning and for your discernment, sir," Flynn finished up.

While Luke pondered the news, everyone shifted. Gabriel Jr. moved toward Charlotte, while Galvin maneuvered in front of her, blocking Gabriel. Charlotte leaned closer to Atarah, grabbing onto her arm. They held onto one another as if their lives depended on it. Their feathery, ivory wings were sloped toward the ground, heavy with sadness. Ben took a step as if to move to Atarah, but a scathing glare from her made him flinch and take a step back. Arick tried to hide his grin. His sister still had fire within her. She knew how to stand up for herself.

Brock and Jared looked warily at the growing formation of rangers before them. While they had been talking, more and more rangers had filed around the clearing. Many still wore massive amounts of clothing piled on them. Any human from the outside would have just seen a cluster of homeless people, concealing their meeting on the inside. How clever.

"A crucial fact was missing from your report, Flynn," Atarah said.

Dropping Charlotte's hand, she took a step closer to Luke. He pivoted and looked at her with a dubious expression before pacing again.

Atarah's wings shook as she spoke. "The 'unknown entity' Flynn mentioned earlier was a Luciferian." Her voice was steady and direct as her message nearly knocked Arick to the ground.

Arick stumbled back, suddenly unsure if he could stand on his own. *A Luciferian!* As of right now, only one Luciferian existed. Matthew.

"We didn't get a close enough look to fully determine it was a Luciferian," Flynn countered. "I said that earlier on the hill because it was what I suspected, but not something I was certain of."

"I am certain," Atarah voiced. "He… It... looked like our father."

Luke whirled around fast and sharpened his gaze upon Atarah. Arick gave a struggling-sounding gasp and nearly doubled over. Brock and Jared came up by his sides, ready to grab onto him if he went down.

Atarah still had no idea.

The thought of having to tell her made his stomach twist into knots. Would she see him for the monster he was born to be? Would she hate him? Luke's gaze shifted to Arick's horrified face as if calculating a difficult math problem.

"Arick?" Atarah said worriedly, coming closer.

She had finally looked back to see he was not doing well. To think she had gotten a close look at Matthew. She never should've been that close to that monster. Breathing became difficult for him at the thought. Arick wondered, in the dark corners of his mind, what he would have done if he had seen the Luciferian. Could he have done anything? Was he so… useless? Pathetic?

No, he thought. *I am just a failure.*

"Arick, are you okay? What's wrong?" Atarah's voice sounded far away.

The darkness closed in on his vision.

"Charlotte!" a voice cried, but Arick was already gone. Succumbed to his own darkness, the unknown.

Chapter 5

Atarah resisted the urge to squirm in her seat. Charlotte had said Arick was fine, but she still had her doubts. What caused him to go down so quickly? When Arick passed out, thankfully, Brock and Jared were already there by his side to catch him. They eased him down while Charlotte examined him. None of the rangers appeared concerned that an Arch Michael warrior fainted. Even Luke didn't appear fazed.

Luke continued walking about as if nothing happened. The rangers stayed in formation as if it was any other day. Atarah wanted to scream at them to get some sort of reaction, but knew that was childish of her.

Atarah glanced at Ben to see if he could catch what Luke was thinking. Ben immediately looked up at Atarah, alerted when his name came through her mind. He must've heard the rest of her thoughts, for he looked at Luke with a concentrated expression, trying to understand his quirky mind. He seemed confused for a long time, while Luke scrutinized Arick's unconscious figure.

After a few minutes, Luke shot up from the ground with a shout, elated. He looked at Arick as if he had figured out something or made up his mind.

"Everyone!" Luke shouted. "We are to celebrate. Let us take our guests to the nethermost!"

Hooting and hollering ensued, followed by them each being surrounded by several rangers. Taken by surprise from their sudden change in demeanor, they were all grabbed into a giant, group bear hug. Squeezed so tightly in the huge group hug, Atarah couldn't move her own arms. Charlotte, Ben, Gabriel, and Arick's soldiers were trapped within this huddle.

Once trapped, the rangers swayed and shouted, as if chanting. The rangers rocked to and fro, yelling a cheer that grew into a battle cry. Despite them all being packed in like sardines, Atarah felt a familiar feeling of weightlessness and heaviness. The world around them started to blur and change quickly as if their eyes could not keep up with what was happening around them.

Just like before, it was over in a matter of seconds. They had been transported to a dark, enclosed space.

"Welcome, Spaceheads," Luke's voice boomed from somewhere in the darkness. "To a place we call home. The Headquarters. The Tabulatum!"

Suddenly, lights brightened their surroundings. They appeared to be in a cave with thousands of entrances and exits—a labyrinth.

Blue and green glowing algae illuminated the entire cave. Atarah looked around, confused and worried about the others. Lost in the crowd of rangers as they all darted in different directions.

"Atarah!" Ben called.

She reached out with her senses and found him immediately. She whirled around for him without thinking. After falling to the ground, Ben grabbed her hand. The contact shocked her. Like before with his touch, electricity shot through her whole body, somehow awakening every cell within her. She knew this sensation was not his power, but from his touch, the effect was still powerful.

For a brief moment, everything was whole, fine, and at peace. Ben stepped closer to her. He wrapped his wings around her and his arms came up to cradle her face. Ben leaned in just a bit as if wanting to kiss her. Atarah jerked her hand back and stumbled away from him, gasping.

Don't be stupid, she thought.

No matter how much time had passed, no matter how much she chanted in her head that she would never forgive him for his betrayal, the effect he had on her was still too powerful. Ben took another step forward, reaching for her. His face was one of torment. He knew the effect he had on her, the pain he had caused.

"Atarah, I—" Ben started, but then slowly dropped his hands. "I will never be able to fully convey how truly sorry I am," Ben whispered in a desperate tone. "I love—"

"Don't," she pleaded.

Her chest tightened around her, making breathing difficult. Tears swelled in her eyes, but she refused to let them fall. She knew he sensed her emotions. She turned away from him, mostly as a way of protection more than pushing him away. She immediately found Charlotte and Gabriel not far from where they stood.

Charlotte sat only a few feet away, looking around in wonder at the labyrinth. Gabriel stood beside her, in apprehension. Stalactites of varying sizes reached down from the ceiling of the cave. Some of the stalagmites, from the ground reaching up to the ceiling, stood taller than Arick. However, what stunned them was the glistening, crystal blue lake before them. One of the light sources came from a small hole at the top of the cave, dozens of meters high. The sun rays poked through. The sun gave an iridescent, mystical look to the cave that filled Atarah with wonder. Many of the rangers took out large hiking packs from different crevices in the cave. The packs contained items like head lamps and different types of clothing..

Dropping their layers of clothing from their backs, they all changed their outfits. Right then and there, no shyness or modesty. The rangers changed into black uniforms of cargo pants and T-shirts before dashing through a large opening.

She attempted to follow the rangers down the tunnel when she remembered Charlotte and Arick. Atarah searched for her brother and his party, ready to go home.

Brock and Jared crouched low beside Arick's unconscious form, several meters away. Galvin, who stood beside them, waved around for them. Once they locked eyes, Atarah reached for Charlotte to draw her attention. Charlotte jumped when she tapped her on the shoulder, but relaxed as she indicated Arick's still form. Gabriel and Ben followed like lost puppies. Galvin moved to the side to allow them room. His shoulders tensed slightly when Gabriel and Ben stepped forward. Atarah ignored them all as she knelt to check on her brother. All his vitals were fine.

"He's still getting some beauty sleep," Brock joked.

Jared gave a humorless chuckle. "Heirs are so high maintenance."

Atarah furrowed her brow and looked between Brock and Jared. "Why on earth did he faint?" she asked, perplexed. "I've never seen him faint before."

Brock and Jared both shrugged, while Galvin shifted his weight, restless.

"Here," Charlotte said gently. Charlotte came beside Atarah. She placed her hands lightly on either side of Arick's head before furrowing her brow in concentration.

Arick flinched and then opened his eyes. His breathing became rapid as his eyes darted around to each of the faces staring down at him.

"What happened?" His voice sounded rough, as if someone had choked him.

"You fainted like a damsel in distress," Brock jeered.

Arick groaned as he sat up. "Give damsels more credit. They can withstand the torture of a corset. I cannot," Arick shot back. He slowly stood and gazed around the cavern. He shuddered.

"What made you feel so….. distressed in the first place?"

Charlotte inquired.

He gave a weak smile, but Atarah didn't miss how his jaw tightened.

"Oh, that." Arick gave a humorless laugh. "I just needed my babysitters."

"Um... I think everyone should turn around and look at this," Gabriel called from behind them. He moved several meters away, hunched around a big alcove.

They all walked over to investigate to see a large pit leading deeper into the cave. The one the rangers travelled down. There were no lights except a faint glow at the bottom. The pit was so dark and buried, the walls seemed like they would close in on you. The echoes of the rangers' cheers told them that they had gone down there, into the cave's depth.

"Who wants to go first?" Arick scoffed.

"I volunteer for Galvin to go first," Brock jested.

Galvin swiveled his head toward Brock with an incredulous expression. He, of course, remained silent as he shook his head.

"Well, you didn't speak up to contest it." Jared patted Galvin on the back.

"It's all up to you, Galvin," Arick joined in.

Atarah and Ben nodded along. Galvin shook his head frantically as Arick pushed him forward. He reached the edge and looked over. His face, surprisingly, paled more as he quickly backed away. Without wings, Atarah wouldn't want to jump off of a ledge either. Galvin turned around and came face to face with Charlotte. He went from pale to a light shade of pink as he looked at her.

"Don't worry, Galvin," Charlotte said gently as she leaned forward. "I will go. I still have my wings with me."

"Then I will go with you." Gabriel stepped closer, blushing.

Galvin blushed too and came closer, looking determined to go now as well. Charlotte reached out her hand to Galvin, who hesitantly grabbed onto her. Gabriel's wings flared, but he remained by her other side.

"Ready?" Gabriel asked.

"As ready as I'll ever be," Charlotte said.

Charlotte glanced at Galvin expectantly. He gave a tentative nod. All three jumped at the same time and plummeted down the abyss. Atarah watched their forms shrink as they fell until they looked like small dots. Apprehension seeped into her mind as she watched her friend disappear. Only her confidence in Charlotte's healing ability kept her at bay. They all watched for a moment in silence.

"Wow," Brock said. "Galvin's silent even when he screams."

A laugh broke out amongst them. Their tense shoulders relaxed for a few seconds, but Ben furrowed his brow in concentration.

"Are you listening to them?" Atarah inquired, her gaze down in the pit.

"Yeah," Ben paused. "Charlotte and Gabriel started to… hover. They didn't need to fly. Something softened the landing for them."

"So, it's safe to take a leap of faith?" Jared said with a raised eyebrow.

Brock and Arick chuckled.

"I'm willing to take the jump," Atarah said.

"You have the comfort of your wings, at least," Arick grumbled.

Brock and Jared jerked their heads from the pit to Atarah.

"I'll go with you!" Brock and Jared volunteered at the same time.

Ben gave them an incredulous look, while Arick simply laughed. Atarah nearly rolled her eyes at the angels. She was surrounded by immaturity.

"We should probably get down there soon. I doubt the rangers will wait for us spaceheads," Atarah said wearily.

"She's right," Ben chimed in. "I can sense them getting restless down there."

It was decided then. They would all jump together. Atarah swallowed the growing fear inside her.

They all crept to the edge and then jumped into the abyss.

Darkness quickly surrounded them. The rush of wind only worsened the sensation. The darkness pressed in on them from all sides. The tiniest bit of light at the bottom created Atarah's only comfort that this would end soon. Atarah attempted to see where the others were, but in vain.

The pit was so dark she couldn't see Ben, who she knew would be close by. She expanded her senses and immediately felt everyone. They were not too far away from her and just as terrified as she was. She still had room for her wings to expand in case their descent did not go as planned. After what felt like a minute of falling, a resistance against her fall pulled. She slowed down as the light at the bottom grew larger. Relief filled her as she slowed. They fell through the opening at the bottom and hovered just above the rock.

They had made it.

Atarah landed on the ground of the cavern. This part of the cavern was similar to what they had seen up top. An elaborate labyrinth with many entrances and exits. Lanterns lined the walls, giving the cavern an eerie, orange glow. She continued to enhance her powers and sensed no end point to this cave. She heard water close by, as well as the rangers. Based on their movements, they were growing agitated, as Ben had said.

Off to the side, Charlotte squirmed under the scrutiny of Gabriel and Galvin's gazes. A silent battle raged between the two males as they glared at each other. Even in dim lighting, she saw Charlotte blushing and uncomfortable at their stand-off. Relief filled Charlotte's face when she caught Atarah's stare. She bounded over to her, as if glad to leave them behind.

"Ready?" Charlotte asked eagerly.

Atarah gave a nod. "I sense the rangers," Atarah said softly. Everyone's attention turned to her. "They are not too far. Just around that corner." Atarah pointed to their left, toward a tunnel with a faint glow and hum.

"Why would the rangers dump us here and then leave?" Gabriel inquired. He and Galvin made their way over, still eyeing each other warily.

"Luke knows we will catch up with them," Ben explained.

Arick looked at Ben skeptically. "Did you get a good read on Luke's mind?" He looked down the tunnel that led to the rangers.

"It… is an interesting mind, I'll give him that. But I am not the best mind reader. I more so see a… general idea of what they are thinking," Ben said hesitantly. "On top of that, his mind looked like this cave. Thoughts going in every direction and some hidden in the darkness of the tunnels."

"No point in waiting any longer," Brock said.

Atarah agreed.

Time to get some answers. They walked down the tunnel with an air of uncertainty. The tunnel was not long, but it was poorly lit. The hum they heard earlier was a cascade of voices that grew louder as they approached. It sounded as if the rangers were in a heated debate about something. Something Atarah wanted to know.

They rounded the corner to find a huge stone amphitheater leading down to a flat stage, where several angels stood. Behind the angels, water descended the cavern walls that were lined with lanterns. This illuminated the space quite well, leaving nothing to the imagination. Atarah turned her attention back to the rangers. She guessed right. They appeared to be in the middle of a heated debate. They entered in the far back of the amphitheater, with a full view.

"It is too dangerous!" one angel shouted.

"We have to think of the repercussions," another voice rang out from the audience.

"Cowards!" yelled another voice.

"We can't just sit back and ignore this new bit of information!"

"It's been centuries since the last Luciferian!"

Luke paced along the stage with a grim expression. His arms were crossed; his wings were out and slightly flared. Without the layered clothes, he wore a simple pair of dark jeans and a fitted, blue, long-sleeve shirt. He was actually quite handsome, Atarah thought in surprise. He cleaned up nicely.

"We should notify the Archs," a voice said from the stage.

Immediately, others responded with boos and jeers.

Atarah drew her eyes away from Luke to see who spoke. She recognized Flynn. Imani stood beside him with her arms crossed. Flynn and Imani both had their wings out, slightly flared.

"Those spaceheads should stick to their own side of the realm!"

"Those uppity fairies—"

Imani flared her wings wide, and the crowd went silent.

"Our brother shall speak his piece." Imani gave a hard stare into the crowd.

No one spoke. Flynn's lips twitched as if he was trying not to smile. He cleared his throat.

"Hear me out, comrades," he began, "Luciferians do not go down easy. If we were to try to take on this level of an enemy on our own, it would cost us many lives." He hesitated. "If legends are even remotely true, this single Luciferian could devastate our whole sector."

Murmurs spread throughout the crowd. Luke, who had been quietly walking around the stage, stopped to look at the crowd. They silenced. He paced again.

"We need reinforcements if we want to keep our deaths to a minimum," Flynn said with a sense of urgency. "I know the pride we have for each other, but I'll be damned if I let my pride be the downfall of any of my comrades!" he said fervently. "I'd rather have a bruised pride in asking for help than have a prideful death."

A moment of silence rang loud as Luke came around. He approached Flynn and Imani, patting Flynn on the back before taking center stage.

"We must celebrate, my friends," Luke said. Atarah glanced at Ben in confusion. Ben shrugged his shoulders, confused as she was. "We must celebrate this time of growth. For we will become stronger."

An angel from the crowd hesitantly stood up.

"Luke," he began. "You are the only one who has ever faced a Luciferian. Do you think we should go to the spaceheads?"

Luke regarded him for a moment before a grin spread on his face. *He is definitely odd,* Atarah thought.

"The spaceheads have already come to us." Luke lifted his hand to point to the back where they all sat. Rows upon rows of angels turned around and stared at them.

"The princes and princesses?" Imani practically sneered.

Atarah resisted the urge to flare her wings. Out of the corner of her eye, she saw Ben, Charlotte, and Gabriel stiffening. Arick's team appeared tense, despite their hidden wings. Arick was the only one at ease under such scrutiny.

"They came, not of their own volition, but because they were needed," Luke continued.

"They are reinforcements?" the angel who stood earlier said. He spoke more out of surprise, but Atarah knew he didn't hold them in high regard either.

Arick stood. Atarah glanced at him, unsure of what he would say.

"Yeah, well." Arick raised his eyebrows. "The oxygen got a little thin up in space, so we thought we would crash down here for a few days or so."

A couple of coughs echoed in the crowd as several tried

to cover their laughs. Even Imani and Flynn cracked small smiles.

Luke smiled brightly and clapped. "My fellow seeker! Please, everyone. Welcome the spaceheads and the seeker for they will be crucial in our next attack."

"Attack?" Gabriel murmured under his breath.

Charlotte visibly paled at Luke's announcement. Brock, Jared, and Galvin looked at Arick in apprehension. Atarah's wings flared. She didn't want to be stuck in anyone else's plan ever again. Ben came closer to her and placed a hand on her shoulder. His action actually calmed the indignation that began to build up within her. Her wings slowly lowered. It was Arick who spoke again.

"Hmmm," Arick started. "I forgot to mention. We are purely for decoration purposes only. Other than that, we don't do much, being spaceheads and all."

Luke stroked his beard and nodded. As if what Arick said was something profound, instead of satirical.

Flynn scoffed and turned to Luke. "Please, Luke," he implored. "You can't honestly see them as anything helpful. Even if they weren't spoiled, royal brats, they're still kids. You can't put kids up against a Luciferian."

"I agree with Flynn on this matter," Imani spoke up. "It is wrong to have them fight alongside us when they will only be in our way."

Atarah shot up, head high and wings slightly flared. Ben stood up alongside her, then Charlotte, followed by Gabriel, Galvin, and lastly, Brock and Jared.

"For once"—Atarah looked at Flynn and Imani and swallowed her anger—"I agree."

Surprise silenced the crowd momentarily. Luke regarded her with seriousness as she continued.

"My friend and I have faced the Abaddon twice now and barely lived. The Luciferian—" She shuddered. "We couldn't even fight because of how powerful he was. He completely debilitated us without having to even lift a finger." She looked up. "All of us have fought difficult battles and have never hesitated. But this... monster… I do not want to see anyone, friend or foe, fall into his hands."

Just as she finished, Luke ventured toward them. He stopped when he reached the steps, glancing back and forth between them all as if assessing them. The rangers sat in a tense silence as they waited for Luke's response.

"It is decided," Luke said.

Atarah tensed. She wasn't sure what Luke meant by his statement.

Luke stared at the rangers seated all around him, hanging on his every word.

"We will engage these powerful demons." Luke looked to the left. "The main priority is to subdue the Abaddon and the Luciferian." Luke looked to the right. "We will notify the Archs in the Spirit realm as a way to gather more information. These demons are moving between realms very comfortably it seems. We need to know why." Luke looked to Arick. "Until then, all I ask from you spaceheads is—" Luke grinned—"Decoration."

"As you say," Flynn and Imani said in unison.

Stomping happened all across the theater as the crowd yelled, "As you say!"

Luke still watched Arick, who paled under his gaze. Atarah glanced between the two of them, confused. Dread coiled in her belly as she realized home would have to wait.

The dust gathered and floated around the air like an invasive pest, persistent in aimless wander and a great annoyance of others in its presence. The small library created stark contrast in a variety of ways. Pale, white walls with perfectly straight columns lined the room. The columns wore no decoration or design. Simple, straight, symmetrical lines adorned the columns. The books along the shelves all bore black covers with white titles typed along the spine. Categorization by subject matter made searching for a general section easy, but searching for a specific book became difficult. All the books looked alike, making the differentiation between titles crucial.

The pitch-black furniture was simple in design and very minimalistic.

Also, very uncomfortable, Noah thought.

He shifted on the hard couch, trying to decipher the text, which proved to be difficult. This library in Mortem made him feel uneasy, especially since he had just come from the grand library in Quaesitor. *At least the Grand Hall had more comfortable seats.* Noah squirmed once again. He had reread the same paragraph for the last half hour now and was still clueless as to what he was reading. He sighed as he dropped his head onto the book in discouragement. How in the realms was he ever going to understand this?

"Stop being lazy," a familiar, spidery-like voice called from the library entrance.

Noah glanced up as Zewal approached his table with more books in his hands. Noah groaned. These particular books looked very thick and wordy.

"I can't read another word," Noah mumbled. "My eyes cross with each letter. It's starting to feel permanent."

"You're a Raphael angel," Zewal drawled. "You'll heal right back up."

Noah swallowed another groan and looked back at Zewal as he sat down. Zewal had been helping Noah in his spare time. In fact, Zewal had been crucial in deciphering much of the information they had gathered. Zewal's demeanor changed toward Noah since the battle. Very minimally, but it was a start. Zewal's pale, featherless wings were relaxed by his sides. He took out his eyeglasses to read, keeping his black eyes down. His pale face almost blended in with the walls. If it weren't for his dark navy hair, he would disappear in the library. Noah tried to be as relaxed, but fidgeted. He struggled around Zewal.

Arick had warmed up to the cold-blooded nature of the Azrael Clan. Noah tried to be at ease with them, but failed. They could not be more opposite. Noah was from the Raphael Clan, which was all about vitality, health, and healing, whereas Zewal from the Azrael Clan represented literal death!

"Stop fidgeting and squirming," Zewal's cold voice carried across the table. "It is distracting, and I need to concentrate."

"These seats are horrendous," Noah complained.

"There is nothing wrong with the seats. Just your discipline," Zewal chided. He turned a page.

With Brock, Jared, and Galvin, researching brought a more lively and bearable atmosphere. Since he returned to Mortem to help with the city's recovery, it had been him and Zewal. During the day, they worked many hours, attending to their duties, meetings, and assignments. Once the day was done, Zewal met him in the library to help him research all he could about Luciferians, halflings, or anything to help Arick. Noah knew that, as word spread to the other Arch heads and angels of the land, Arick would have a huge battle to face.

Noah guessed the Arch heads would gather soon to discuss what would happen to Arick now that they knew of his parentage. He wanted to do everything he could to argue in Arick's stead for him. To build up a solid case for him and plead before the Heads to not harm him. Zewal wanted the same, to protect their friend. To help Arick stay alive. Until then, they created this uneasy truce between them, reading in the library late at night, searching for anything remotely helpful.

Very quietly, to say the least. Over the past few days, nearly weeks, Zewal said a handful of words to him. Most of the time, he reprimanded Noah. If Zewal had found anything useful for Arick, he wrote it down. By the end of the night, he gave his notes to Noah and then left for bed.

Noah grimaced at the thought of 'bed' because the Azrael's lifestyle was different from other regions. Especially their sleep cycle. Many angels in the Vallis remained awake from dusk until dawn, whereas everyone else functioned from dawn until dusk. The change in sleep cycle had been difficult for Noah. Now that demons were no longer a threat, the Azrael angels went about their normal nighttime routines, guiding lost souls from the different realms. While they were up all night, they slept all day, effectively avoiding the blistering, desert sun.

Meanwhile, Noah had to trudge out during the day to lead his soldiers between Campis Secretum and the Vallis region to assist in resettlement. He was beyond exhausted. His heavy eyelids threatened to shut completely for the night. When he sent his troops home, he would get more sleep. He got up from his chair and stretched for a moment. He couldn't fall asleep when he was so close to deciphering this last chapter.

"Don't become useless now," Zewal said, not looking up from his book. He turned another page.

"I am just a little sleepy is all," Noah grumbled as he stretched. "What's the title of that book?" He became curious as he tried to read around Zewal's shoulder.

Zewal sighed. "It is titled *The Hierarchy and Structure of the Demon Realm* by an unknown author." his voice sounded as tired as Noah felt.

"Learned anything new?" Noah asked, trying to end this silence. He was bound to fall asleep tonight if he didn't have some sort of conversation to keep him going.

"Much of it is dense and contradictory at times."

"Contradictory? In what way?"

"Are you always this loquacious at night?" Zewal said with a hint of annoyance.

"I am just trying to stay awake," Noah said with a bite.

He was slightly irritated as well. But his frustration was more because he was tired, whereas Zewal… Well, it just seemed to be part of his personality.

Zewal sighed again and turned the page. A moment of silence echoed between them. After a few minutes, Zewal spoke again, but this time, his voice sounded less cold.

"The book explains about how unnatural demons are, but then goes on about how crucial they are when it comes to the balance of the realms."

"The balance of the realms?" Noah pondered the question more for himself than to Zewal.

"It also explains how a demon matures, in a way," Zewal said hesitantly.

"How a demon grows up?" Noah said, surprised. He never thought of demons in that way. He thought they were just… there.

"No," Zewal said firmly. "Demons do not grow up, yet they are born." Zewal furrowed his brows together. "I am still trying to understand it all."

Zewal looked up from his book to analyze him.

"What have you learned?" Zewal asked coolly. "You must know more than me at this point."

Noah sighed and ran a hand through his hair. He went back to his chair and the stack of papers he had collected.

"It is just as confusing for me as it is for you. Very few angels have tried to learn about demons, let alone understand them." Noah flipped over one of his pages. "One page talks about the amount of suffering demons go through to become demons, and then the next page is about how demons are actually agents of good deeds." Noah scoffed. "But if there are demons who do good, I can use that to help with Arick's case." Noah said the last part, not really paying attention to his speech, now too engrossed in the page.

Zewal reacted, nonetheless. "*Arick is not a demon,*" Zewal hissed viciously. His wings flared.

Noah flinched as Zewal's black eyes constricted to focus on him. His wings flared at the anger in Zewal's eyes.

"What do you think he is then?" Noah said, more out of curiosity than indignation.

Zewal's wings shuddered. "I don't know," he said in a calmer tone. "But there is no way he is a demon or halfling." Zewal turned back to his pages. "He can't be," he nearly whispered.

Noah glanced down at the book Zewal had been reading. An epiphany occurred to him. This whole time, Zewal had been searching for ways to prove Arick was *not* a demon, while he had been looking for ways to spare his life, even if he was a demon. Would Zewal still help him if Arick was a demon? Or condemn him? Noah pursed his lips. He couldn't be picky about who helped Arick or how. Whatever kept him alive was what mattered most. Noah went back to his own book, feeling more alert.

Noah read further about Seraphim and Cherubim. Angels had a hierarchy, so did the demons. In fact, the hierarchy system that demons practiced mirrored their own. Noah moved through a few pages, searching for a keyword. Luciferian. Noah remembered back to when he asked Joshua what was known of Luciferians. He had pursed his lips in frustration at the memory.

"The few books we have on Luciferians are some of the most difficult books to decipher. Their authors wrote the information in a code to limit its knowledge," Joshua had explained to him a week earlier.

"Is there anyone who has been able to understand the books?" Noah asked in desperation.

Joshua sighed and gently shook his head. "There were a few who made breakthroughs in deciphering the text. But whenever one of the scholars finished the entire text, they often tried to destroy their notes so no one else could decipher it." Joshua looked at Noah with a grim expression. "They did not want anyone else to learn what they had learned. Not even themselves. A few went mad from what they had learned from the book. A couple even committed suicide."

"Is the knowledge that dangerous?" Noah asked incredulously.

Joshua gave a grim nod. "Be careful what you uncover." Joshua patted him on the shoulder. "Ignorance can be bliss."

Noah shook his head slightly, as if to shake away the memory. There had to be a way. But now, Noah would go mad if he didn't decipher these texts.

From his research, Luciferians were angels, high up in the hierarchy, who had been turned. There was not one specific way to turn an Archangel. However, turning an angel happened through any method of pure torment over an extended period of time. The length of time was nonspecific, just like the type of torment. However, what caught his eye was how Luciferians were not considered demons, but almost as a guide for demons. One page described a Luciferian like a shepherd leading a flock of sheep. Another book explained them as god-like creatures that had no mercy for anything.

A caring but deadly being. Noah shook his head in confusion. He moved onto another book. Upon the first page of the new book, an Abaddon was sketched. Noah twitched, uneasy. He couldn't believe Charlotte had been up against such a powerful demon. Abaddon drained powers from their opponents and absorbed them as their own. Once an angel's powers were depleted, the Abaddon drained the angel's life force, slowly and painfully.

Noah moved on to another page. The next page was in a language Noah had never seen before. He flipped the page back again, confused by the change. The odd symbols were still there. He tried to skip a few pages ahead and saw the pages were blank. *What happened to the rest of the book?* Noah flipped through the pages in confusion. Beyond the page with the strange language, there was nothing.

"I can hear you thinking in confusion." Zewal sighed. His eyes were down, looking at his own book. "What is it this time?"

Noah ignored his tone and swallowed his pride. He needed to ask for help.

"Have you ever seen this language?" Noah passed the book to Zewal.

He sighed as he took the book and regarded the page. His black eyes darted back and forth quickly before looking up at Noah.

"What do you know?" Noah asked, resisting the urge to look away from his eyes.

Zewal frowned slightly. "This is the language of the dead." Zewal's frown deepened. "Where did you get this book?"

"This batch of books came from this library and from Joshua's collection."

Zewal scoffed. "Of course from Joshua," he murmured. "Very few can read this language. The ones who can are said to have the 'soul-seeing' eyes."

"Soul-seeing eyes? What does that mean?"

"It is someone who has the ability to see the soul of the writer." Zewal turned the page. "The writer is dead, which is why this is in the language of the dead and the spirit of the writer writes it down."

Noah furrowed his brow. "I don't understand."

"Imagine I rub my hand on this table." He lifted his hand. "Some of my essence was left on the table. The same goes for a soul. The writer left his or her essence on these pages." Zewal turned the pages. "We just cannot see it. But these pages are probably filled with passages."

"You mean to tell me that a ghost wrote in this book?" Noah said skeptically.

Zewal continued to flip through the empty pages.

"A very elementary way of saying it, but yes." Zewal went back to the first page. "I imagine any Raziel angel would love to get their hands on the knowledge in this book."

Noah shook his head. "But how can we see this page of the language, but not the rest?"

Zewal went back to the page with the strange symbols.

"This page is a test to unlock the rest of the passage. Understand this and you will be able to read the rest."

"Can you read it? You've seen the souls of the dead," Noah said hopefully.

Zewal's lips tightened, and his wings flared slightly.

"You think every Azrael angel knows the language of death because we guide souls to the afterlife?" His voice was ice-cold again.

Noah sputtered and blushed.

"I didn't mean—"

"Of course, you didn't." Zewal looked up. "Just like not every Raphael angel can heal someone else."

Noah looked down, as his face flushed. "I apologize," he said quietly. "It is wrong to make assumptions or generalizations of any clan."

Zewal's wings relaxed, and he moved his gaze down.

"Um, also…" Noah said hesitantly. Zewal turned his head to show he was listening. "You don't need to keep your gaze down."

Zewal raised his eyebrows, but kept his gaze down.

"You are at least perceptive," Zewal murmured. "I am used to it."

"Used to keeping your gaze down?" Noah said, surprised. "It is normal to look into other people's eyes when having a conversation."

Zewal nodded as he spoke.

"However, many angels do not feel comfortable looking into an Azrael angel's eyes. It makes them squirm. Our eyes are so black that angels say they cannot see our soul. Or question if we even have a soul. So, to make them comfortable, many Azrael angels will avoid eye contact."

"You don't need to do that with me," Noah replied, trying to add confidence to his voice.

Zewal looked at him then. "Feeling brave?"

"No, I feel extremely uncomfortable." He cleared his throat. "But that's my problem and not yours. You can't change your eyes any more than you can change how I feel. Only I can change that."

It was hard to describe the look on his face, but something shifted in Zewal's black eyes as he regarded Noah. Almost as if he had gained some respect. Zewal gave a nod before returning the book back to Noah.

"I do know one person who may be able to read that passage," Zewal spoke. His voice sounded warm.

"Really? Who?" Noah asked eagerly.

Zewal grimaced as if the thought actually pained him.

"My mother."

Noah felt as if ice water had been dumped on him. Noah had not seen Fatima since that fateful day when she told everyone of Arick's true heritage.

"How has she been?"

Zewal sighed and closed the book.

"She has requested to be left alone by almost everyone except my father. Only he is allowed in," Zewal said in a soft tone. "She was never really a social person to begin with, but now she truly loathes the company of others."

"What about you and your sister?" Noah asked, searching his eyes.

"I've been so busy with our people, so I've hardly given her much time." Zewal's wings drooped. "She wants me to visit, but… I… can't just yet." He looked up. "Tariel visits her regularly, though. Ask her if she is willing to decipher these texts for you." Zewal stood up and moved to leave the small library.

"Wait!" Noah called. Zewal paused at the door with his back still to him. "Why can't you ask her?"

Zewal's wings trembled. "If it wasn't for me, my mother would not have been captured in the first place." Zewal half turned his head. "I can't see her yet," he whispered before closing the door on Noah.

Noah fell back down to his unbearably hard seat and ran his hands through his hair. What was he to do? Would this text be helpful or just another puzzle for him to solve? So much uncertainty filled his head for a moment that he felt defeated. Overwhelmed by how little he knew and how helpless he felt.

He sighed and stood back up. He could not give in yet. He gathered the book and a few papers and made his way out of the library. The white, smooth walls of Sewall's house did not bear any pictures, plants, or artwork. The walls only held the occasional small, black bookshelf, similar to those in the library, or a black-framed mirror. The colors of the home consisted of black, white, or gray. Noah learned that Azrael households typically were minimalistic and held few colors. Most homes were white on the outside to deflect the heat of the sun. However, during the night, they preferred the dark furniture to help keep the home warm. Even the guest room they had offered Noah held a black, stone bed frame with a white duvet. The furniture consisted of a black desk, a dresser, and a single mirror. Noah declined the offer, stating he should stay with his soldiers.

Though, one of these days, he wanted to sneak in a plant or painting of some kind to add color to this eerie home. *Maybe I'll "gift" Zewal or Sewall a painting,* Noah thought to himself. He chuckled as he imagined Zewal's sneer at whatever he would bring.

Noah turned his attention to the papers in his hand. The notes looked extensive and full of so much knowledge, and yet it was only scratching the surface. Noah had learned more than he had ever thought he would about the realms in the past few weeks. That the three realms included the demon realm, Spirit realm, and human realm. Some Raziel scholars had theorized that the realms made up the Trinity, while others theorized something different. The demon realm was vast and larger than the Spirit realm and human realm combined. In fact, the magnitude of the demon realm was so large, many scholars thought angels did not know the complete size of the demon realm.

The variety of demons were so diverse and immense. The ones he had battled were only a small portion of the population. The demons that had been on the mountain a few weeks ago were mere foot soldiers. Weak and disposable. Some demons were ancient and powerful. The records were all over the place describing the types of powerful demons, and others disputed if they even existed.

Noah was deep in his own thoughts when a movement from the corner of his eye caught his attention. Tariel's black tunic trailed behind her as she turned the corner. Just who he was looking for.

"Wait!" Noah called out.

He cut toward the hallway Tariel had just gone down. Her tall frame made her easy to spot. A white scarf was wrapped around her head, hiding her dark navy hair. Her pale, leathery wings were relaxed by her side as she turned around to look at him in mild curiosity. If her brother was a temperamental snake, she was a clever desert fox. Not as cold as her brother, but just as calculating. He had never paid much attention to her, nor she to him, until Arick showed up.

She regarded him with a bored expression, while he caught his breath. Her black eyes never looked at him directly, but around him. Her tall, wiry frame no longer looked awkward, like a little girl getting used to her size, but sleek and elegant. She was definitely her own woman now.

"I need your help with something," Noah said quietly.

Tariel raised her eyebrows, but did not look directly at him.

"I need help deciphering a text within this book." Noah

held out the book before her.

Tariel scrunched her forehead in disdain.

"I am not like my brother." Tariel's smooth voice carried finality. "I have no desire to decipher text." She turned to walk away, but Noah stopped her.

"No, wait." He moved to step in front of her. He had to tilt his head up to meet her eyes.

"I need your mother's help, really." Noah lifted the book once more. "This book has a hidden text that only someone with 'soul-seeing' eyes can read. Zewal said your mother could read this text." Tariel's face looked passive and expressionless, so Noah continued. "The information in this text could help Arick."

At that, her face softened, and her wings vibrated a little. She held out her hand.

"May I see this book?" Her voice sounded lighter. Noah quietly handed the book over. The book looked almost small in her long hands as she flipped the pages over.

Her face did not give much away, but she paused when she reached the page with the strange language. She furrowed her eyebrows as if in concentration. Noah wasn't sure if she was aware that she had begun moving. Tariel walked toward the end of the hall, absentmindedly waving him to follow. Noah followed quickly. He noticed the door before she did.

He scurried in front and opened the door before she ran into it. He looked into the room to see they were in what seemed to be a large sitting area. The furniture was customarily black, of course, but what surprised Noah was that the far wall was made of glass. Beyond the glass was a large cavern. On the far side of the cavern stood a large, pale Head Tree. Several tunnels led to and from the Head Tree.

The sound of running water brought Noah closer to the glass until he was pressed up against it. A river flowed from one of the caverns down toward the tree. The darkness of the cavern was held back by luminous, blue light that glowed like star-light. The Head Tree appeared to glow from the blue light. It was so beautiful that Noah could do nothing but stand in awe of the cavern's beauty.

"First time seeing our Head Tree?" Tariel asked, looking up briefly from the book.

Noah nodded. "Yes," he nearly whispered, still in awe of the beauty.

"The caverns are… not a place to take lightly," Tariel continued. She flipped a page over as she spoke. "There are many mysteries… or rather, creatures that lay asleep in the caverns. Creatures that we are not allowed to disturb."

"Creatures?" Noah said in bewilderment. "What kind of creatures? Where do the caverns lead to? Why didn't you show me earlier?" Noah's wings hummed slightly in excitement. He had heard about the infamous Maze of Uncertainty, but few had fully navigated the cave, so little was known about it.

Tariel continued to concentrate on the book, but she answered anyway.

"Angels from other regions rarely come to visit, let alone explore some of the most dangerous parts of our capital." Tariel flipped another page. "After all, it is not like I know much about Silva other than the abundance of autumn leaves that grow there. Even then, I have only seen pictures illustrated in a book about Silva. Never been there to see it with my own eyes."

"Maybe this needs to change," Noah said grimly.

"Good luck." Tariel nearly scoffed. "The regions have not been on good terms for a couple of decades now. One thing I have learned so far as an heir"—Tariel looked up—"is that change is hard."

"But necessary," Noah countered. He regarded Tariel for a moment as he pondered her statement. "How will we grow if we do not change?"

Tariel clicked her tongue.

"You'd be surprised how many creatures would rather die than change. And we are no exception." She went back to the book. "I imagine that you did not like it when Arick came into your life because it was a massive change."

Noah's wings twitched. He had despised Arick when he had first met him. Now he was doing everything in his power to help him. Nonetheless, all of it took time. The time to get to know him, learn from him, understand him, and to feel empathy for him.

"Time is change's ultimate ally," Noah said softly.

Tariel scoffed as she turned a page. "For your sake, I hope you are right."

Noah jumped as he noticed what Tariel was doing. Since they had entered the room, she had been flipping through the pages. Flipping through them as if she was actually reading them.

"Tariel! Are you reading those passages?"

"No," she drew out the word with sarcasm. "I just like to stare at blank pages as a way to reflect upon my own soul." She glanced up at him with a ghost of a smile. "Yes, I am reading the passages."

Noah rolled his eyes. "You and Arick are perfect for each other."

Tariel turned to a bright shade of red and for once looked speechless. She turned her face back to the book, still blushing.

"What does the book say? Can you understand it?" Noah asked fervently. Would this finally give him something useful to work with?

"The soul who wrote this was in anguish." Tariel turned another page. "I think this was written by a Luciferian," Tariel said hesitantly.

"A Luciferian? That's perfect! We can get valuable intel about how they operate, and this could help us with Arick! What else does it say?" Noah's eyes went back and forth between Tariel's face and the blank pages.

"Um." Tariel squirmed a little under his scrutiny. "It is talking about the trials and oppression. I haven't gotten that far—"

A bell rang in the distance. The bell signaled that dawn was upon them. Noah groaned. The night was over, and he would have to endure another grueling day of work with his soldiers.

"I have to go and get my soldiers ready for training. But tonight, can we meet again after you've had some more time to read further into the book? I think this will be crucial knowledge for us."

Tariel glanced up at him with those pitch-black eyes.

"I will try my best." She looked hesitant for a moment. "Also, Noah, please do not tell my father what I am doing for you."

"Sure, but why?"

"Fear has changed my father," Tariel said carefully. "Fear is... a strange concept to Azrael angels and we do not react well to it. Especially my family."

Noah did not quite understand, but nodded all the same. He would have an easier time meeting up with Tariel than her mother anyway.

Another bell signaled. This time the bell meant the sun was over the horizon. Time for Noah to start his daily tasks. He rubbed his eyes once more.

"All right. Agreed. I will look for you tonight." Noah started to walk toward the door, but paused when he reached for the handle. "Oh, and Tariel." She looked up from the book again. "Thank you. I truly appreciate it."

An ever so tiny smile came to her lips, but she said nothing. She returned to her book in deep concentration. Noah closed the door and quickly left the estate. As he flew to the encampment of his troops, he wondered again about Tariel's parting request. Was it right to involve her? Or would this be too dangerous?

Chapter 6

Desert sand was within every corner and crevice on Elijah's body. Occasionally, the wind picked up and whipped the sand around, like sending shards of glass in every direction. Elijah adjusted his shemagh once more, trying to keep his eyes from getting stung.

Behind him, in the distance, stood the magnificent city of Chrysi Poli. Shining in the bright morning sun, the city was a beacon. An oasis. Tropical trees surrounded the city as the Dark River traveled through the city.

The Dark River descended from the snow of the Living Mountains in Belli Causa. The river grew large as it left the Belli Causa and flowed into several neighboring regions. Providing substances for the Lanua, Arena, and Campis Secretum regions, the river had become crucial for many angels, including Elijah. He turned away from the city to see the Dark River flowing further into the desert before him.

"Are you ready?" A deep voice beside him spoke.

Elijah pivoted to address Mikael. "As ready as I will ever be," he murmured.

Mikael stood before him in a white tunic and shemagh. The clothing was breathable in this hot climate and comfortable to move around in. They both had been given a change of clothes by Amos, the young Head Arch of the Selaphiel Clan. Elijah's heart had ached for the new Arch Head. Though he was no boy, Amos was still young and reminded Elijah of

Noah in some ways. To be placed as the head of a clan from the violent passing of one's parents was nothing to take lightly.

Elijah glanced up at Mikael once more, thinking back to what led them here. Mikael had sent a request to Elijah asking for help in tracking down the Abaddon that had attacked their daughters. The last sighting of the Abaddon had been outside of the Lanua region, following the Dark River into the Arena region. Elijah had been shocked that Mikael had asked for his help, even after he had schemed to marry Atarah away from him. Elijah kept glancing nervously at Mikael since he had arrived in Chrysi Poli.

This was the first time Elijah had been face-to-face with Mikael in months, since the emergency summit meeting. Then Elijah had hated Mikael with a passion. Now... Elijah was not sure what to make of Mikael anymore. He had seen him as his enemy for so long, working with him felt awkward, to say the least.

They had met at the city center in Chrysi Poli and were greeted by Amos upon arrival. Amos had given them an update on the last his troops saw of the Abaddon, as well as the bizarre disappearance of the demon army that caused the death of the last Selaphiel Head. The only thing left by the army had been a dark, bitter, unknown substance.

Amos gave them food, clothes, and shelter for the night before they headed out this morning. Mikael had said very little other than sharing his reports from the southern regions. The majority of his troops were traveling north to return home, while a few squads spread out to every region to assist in rebuilding cities and towns, recovering captured angels, and defending against any straggling demons in the area. While the large holes in the south were closed, small openings still remained in different parts of the regions.

"I promise you, Elijah," Mikael said quietly. "You have nothing to fear from me."

"What makes you say that?"

Mikael nodded toward him. "You haven't relaxed your wings since you arrived last night."

Elijah's wings twitched and he tried to relax them.

"Given the circumstances leading up to this moment, a little tension is normal," Elijah retorted.

Mikael gave a small smile. "I suppose so." His face turned somber again. "Thank you for coming. I truly appreciate it."

Elijah gave an uneasy laugh. "I was surprised that the great and powerful Mikael actually needed help."

"Against an Abaddon, absolutely," he said seriously. "It is not a demon to take lightly. Even thought about involving a Cherubim."

"I thought Abaddons were wiped out by you Michael angels."

Mikael gave a grimace. "So did I."

"Were you not the last one to fight one before this one appeared?"

Mikael looked at him then. "I believe this one is the same one I fought all those years ago. I think it must have survived the fight and healed its wounds back in the demon realm."

"Wouldn't you have burned its carcass to be sure?" Elijah said, confused. Every angel knew to burn a demon's carcass.

Mikael's wings flared slightly. "I left that task to my brother Matthew." Mikael said quietly, but this time, his tone possessed an icy undertone.

Elijah's wings flared out too. For so many years, he had been angry at Mikael for taking his daughter—for being a monster—when really, it had been Matthew terrifying his daughter at night. And himself. For years, Ava had been scared of him, for what he might have done if he had found out about Arick. In all fairness, her fears were not unfounded. Without a doubt, he would have killed Arick and taken Ava away from the place where she probably felt most safe—in Campis Secretum guarded by the one angel who could challenge Matthew in battle, Mikael.

"Mikael…" Elijah said, trying to soften his tone. His anger from the past had gripped him, but now he tried to move past it.

Mikael looked at him and waited patiently.

"Thank you," Elijah whispered. "From the bottom of my heart. Thank you for all that you've done for Ava." Elijah struggled with anger at himself that he could do very little for Ava and in the end, he had made things worse.

Mikael came up and put his hand on his shoulder.

"You have a strong daughter, Elijah," Mikael said softly. "Despite all of the pain, I am happy to have her in my life and I wouldn't trade it for all of the realms."

"I am sorry about Atarah…" Elijah started, but he didn't know how to end his sentence.

Mikael shook his head and gave a proud smile. "You'll have to answer to my daughter yourself. She's a force to reckon with all on her own."

Mikael moved away from Elijah and walked further toward the vast desert.

"Until then, we have to focus on catching up with the Abaddon."

"Why would it follow the river from Urbs Antiqua? Demons typically don't like the water," Elijah murmured as he gazed south.

"I'm not sure, which is why we need to find out." He gazed toward the south as well.

Traveling south would bring them to Campis Secretum toward the Coal Mountains in Joshua's region. Mikael expanded his wings completely and took off into the sky. Elijah quickly followed. The desert wind and sand greeted him instantly. Despite the chaotic sound of the wind, Elijah could still hear Mikael when he spoke.

"Stay sharp, Elijah," Mikael yelled, but did not turn around. "Our children were lucky to survive against a demon like this one. Now that it is heading for Josh's region, it will be able to mimic any Raziel angel's ability to conceal itself through illusion and apparitions."

"It can drain us of our powers and our life force, correct?"

"Yes."

"Wouldn't an Azrael angel be better for this job? Sewall could probably drain the demon faster than any fight we could put up," Elijah inquired.

"Sewall would be the worst opponent against an Abaddon. Any Azrael angel would be."

"What? Why?" Elijah asked incredulously.

"An Azrael's power would drain the demon, but the demon in turn would drain the angel right back. This would go on and on, back and forth until one of them tires out. If the Azrael angel tires, the Abaddon will overpower them through physical strength," Mikael explained.

Of course. Azrael angels, while incredibly powerful, relied entirely on their powers against demons, as opposed to Michael angels, who were physically strong and had overwhelming power.

Elijah glanced forward at Mikael's flying form. He still asked for help to go up against this demon. Elijah wondered what type of Arch Mikael had been all along. He thought back to the reports he had been given by the other Archangel Heads about this Abaddon. This had been the first one they had seen in such a long time. Elijah had nearly forgotten what he knew about them. From Malachi, he had written that the Abaddon had come from the south, attacking the Uriel Head Tree with such force he could do nothing except watch in horror. The demon army appeared suddenly and swiftly, overwhelming them, decimating the once gorgeous city of Aquam Caput.

Joshua's report said they had not seen or heard of the Abaddon until it attacked Aquam Caput. Gabriel Sr. had seen the Abaddon leave his region, but had been too overwhelmed by other demons to even have a chance to send word out.

Also, more of his soldiers had been disappearing. Otherwise, there had been no reports of the Abaddon attacking. Just the Head Tree of Aquam Caput and the capital city of Sanctum. For such a powerful demon with a bottomless appetite, one would think it would have attacked nearly everything in sight. The demon had traveled from the Vallis region all the way to Belli Causa with only two attacks?

Matthew must have a tight grip of control over such a powerful demon as an Abaddon, which begged the question: how powerful was Matthew that he could control so many demons? Powerful ones, at that. He was sure Mikael had asked the same question as well. Did Matthew become stronger while in the demon realm? Was there any part of him that was… his old self? Would they run into him on this journey south?

Elijah glanced back at the Head Arch of the Michael Clan and yelled, "Mikael!"

He veered around slightly to look back at him, but kept his speed. He raised his eyebrow in question.

"Will we be enough if we come across Matthew?"

Mikael slowed and frowned slightly.

"I am not sure. My goal for now was to gather more information about him before engaging with him. I have no idea how powerful he has become. The fact that he has control over an Abaddon speaks volumes about his strength." Mikael looked back at him. "We can take the Abaddon, but I am not sure about Matthew."

"Have you heard nothing about him since the battle in the mountains?" Elijah said with some surprise. Surely, Amos or Joshua's soldiers would have reported something by now.

"Yes, sadly." Mikael's frown deepened. "The last report came from Luke, of all angels."

"Luke?" Elijah asked, baffled. "The eccentric in the human realm?"

Mikael gave a grim nod.

"He reported that Matthew appeared before our daughters in the human realm and nearly took them. Two of his soldiers intervened, and Matthew disappeared. None of them had any idea how dangerous Matthew had become, except Luke."

"He was in the human realm?" His wings faltered. He had sent Charlotte and Atarah there to be farther away from danger, and yet he ended up putting them right at danger's doorstep!

"Once Luke heard what happened, he brought all his active team members together." Mikael seemed hesitant to continue.

Sweat started to drip from Elijah's body. It had been from the desert sun, but now it was out of concern for his daughter and granddaughter.

"He requested that we allow our children to stay there to help," Mikael finished. Sweat started to form along his brow, but he did not look tired in the slightest.

Elijah's eyes widened in outrage. He sped up and came in front of Mikael, forcing them to both stop their flight and hover in the air.

"You want our children to stay in an outside world, fighting against an enemy that is far too strong for them?!" Elijah's voice grew louder as he spoke. His wings vibrated as they fought to keep him up in the air.

Mikael looked infuriatingly calm before him.

"They may be safer in the human realm, Elijah."

"Bring them back NOW, Mikael!" Elijah bellowed.

Mikael remained calm, angering him further.

"Are you not scared for them? How can you let them stay there?"

"Of course, I am scared!" Mikael spoke back with strained control. "I kept my children locked up in Belli Causa for their whole lives out of fear—fear of what Matthew would do to them—especially Arick." Mikael clenched his fists as if trying to regain his composure. "Hearing Atarah took on an Abaddon and nearly died"—Mikael looked at him with pain in his eyes—"and watching Arick find out the truth about Matthew, I realized that my children do not need protecting. They need someone who will teach and prepare them for life. Not dictate or control their lives."

Elijah was stunned quiet for a moment as he listened to Mikael's words. Fear was still present, but outrage dwindled away.

"When Atarah spoke up at the Summit meeting all those months ago, it was then I realized they were not children to control anymore. They are their own people who need control of their own lives, which scared me more. But I couldn't be the parent who took that away from them." Mikael looked at Elijah.

A sharp feeling stabbed him in the chest. How many choices had he and Elizabeth taken away from Noah and Charlotte? The very reason they were in the human realm was because of him. Fear for his children's lives was still very present, but Mikael was right.

"If it is any consolation, I see that they are safer in the human realm. The rangers are warrior angels from every region, and they all have different abilities. They are trained in battle, while also familiar with the human world. Even demons have to honor the rules of concealment in the human realm. With an army of rangers beside them, even Matthew would not do anything too reckless against them," Mikael explained.

"Helps… only a little."

Mikael gave a knowing smile. "Having children is never easy."

"Elizabeth and I were not always like this," Elijah nearly whispered.

"Ava spoke about how loving and carefree both of you had been when she was growing up." Mikael frowned. "I was sorry to see the pain that hiding Ava caused you both."

Elijah scoffed, but said nothing. The sun still blazed down upon them as they hovered in the sky of the barren desert.

They were losing daylight.

"We need to hurry if we are to make it to the Coal Mountains," Elijah spoke softly.

Mikael nodded once more as if understanding Elijah's need to move on. Talking about his kids left him feeling completely raw.

Mikael spread his wings wide and gave a powerful flap, propelling him forward. Elijah followed his pace. He had to flap his wings twice as hard as Mikael, but he was able to keep up. A golden, dry sea seemed to be endless, but he knew they were heading in the right direction toward the southern mountains.

As they flew, Elijah thought about how he would tell Elizabeth about the Luciferian. He had gone to her room to say goodbye and found her to be withdrawn and cold. She had sat by the window, looking out with unseeing eyes and a blank page from her journal in her hand. A pen dangled in her other hand as if forgotten.

Charlotte glanced around her, uncertain of the angels who sat close by. Luke had agreed to take on the Abaddon and Luciferian, but with their help. Charlotte suppressed a shudder. She did not want to feel either demon's eyes on her again. Gabriel's wings twitched at her tension. His ever-watchful eyes continuously glanced at her from the sides. Galvin had silently refilled her drink, while she had briefly looked away. Gabriel sat to her left, while Galvin sat to her right. Atarah was directly across from her. The seats by her were taken up by Arick, who looked pale still, and Ben.

They were still in the amphitheater. Angels milled about in different groups as they ate. Rangers handed out bags of food to everyone and sat down to eat. They stayed in the back of the amphitheater, away from everyone. However, many of the rangers stared at them. Some in disdain, others with mere curiosity. Luke brought more attention to them since he 'volunteered' them to help against the Abaddon and Luciferian.

Atarah glanced up as if sensing her gaze. Her striking, mixed colored eyes squinted slightly, asking a silent question. Charlotte tried to make her gaze look as pleading as possible for them to switch seats. To her embarrassment, Atarah gave a small smile as if amused by her awkward predicament. Both male angels beside her appeared determined to outdo one another. Even now, after Galvin filled her drink, Gabriel added more food onto her plate. Each of them gave each other a tense glares, making Charlotte feel more uncomfortable with each passing minute. She wished for many things. She wished both of them would stop. She wished she could sit by Atarah. Wished she could return home and feel safe. Her longing must have shone in her eyes for Atarah's teasing smile turned into a face of concern.

"Do you want to go home, Charlotte?" Atarah echoed her thoughts.

Though she had spoken to her directly in a hushed tone, Charlotte felt all too aware of everyone listening, including the rangers.

"Just say the word, and I will take you back," Gabriel whispered to her.

She swallowed her irritation at his statement. Why couldn't he have done that before all this happened? Now the leader of the rangers expected their help against such horrible monsters. She clenched her fists. She couldn't be someone other people needed to look after. Also, she didn't want to see her mother again.

"No," Charlotte said softly. She looked at Atarah. "Can we practice after the meal?"

Atarah grinned and gave a small nod. She understood her need to get stronger, faster, better.

"We may as well join you," Arick spoke up beside Atarah.

He glanced at Brock, Jared, and Galvin.

"We are going up against the toughest Michael angel in the realms, so we will need to get stronger," Arick murmured.

Atarah froze and her wings twitched.

"What do you mean the toughest Michael angel?" Atarah glanced curiously at Arick.

Charlotte peered up as well. Atarah had told her that he had been acting strange ever since they had reunited.

Arick rubbed his face and sighed.

"I guess I need to tell you." He looked up to see everyone staring at him. Ben, Gabriel, Atarah, and Charlotte all regarded him, waiting.

"Tell me what?" Atarah asked. Her voice lowered in suspicion.

"The Luciferian is…" he sighed. "Matthew, the first heir to the House of Michael, before our father."

"Our father's older brother?" Atarah's eyebrows furrowed. Her wings twitched in uncertainty. "How is that possible?"

Ben placed his hand on her lap, which relaxed her.

"We were told our uncle died in battle," Atarah said as if that settled everything.

Arick shook his head somberly.

"The battle of Mount Hermon?" Gabriel nearly whispered.

Ben nodded softly.

"It was said that he drove through enemy lines, cutting down all the demons who were in his path. But he was swarmed quickly. Father and the other soldiers saw him go down while in the demon realm. But before Father could retrieve his body, the portal between the realms closed. So, they were never able to recover his body and assumed he was dead," Arick explained. "Father didn't know he was alive and turned into a Luciferian until it was too late."

Charlotte's eyes widened in shock at this information.

Someone who was an Archangel heir had been turned! No wonder he had been so powerful when they had met him. She glanced at Atarah, who looked at Arick in disbelief. Atarah shook her head.

"How—" She stopped. "Why—" Stopped again. "Wouldn't—" She closed her mouth as if at a loss for words.

"Wouldn't Father have told us the truth?" Arick finished. He looked away from his sister. He rubbed his face again and covered his eyes with his hand.

"Matthew appeared before our mom and… forced himself on her." Arick's jaw clenched. He hunched over and held his face within his hands, but he continued. "Father came in right after, and that was how he learned that he was alive and a Luciferian. Mom became pregnant with me, but to hide the pregnancy from the other Archs and from Matthew, father married our mother and kept us away in Belli Causa. He didn't know when Matthew would be back, and by then, all the other Archs had dubbed him the 'Great Betrayer' and no longer trusted him." Arick unclenched his jaw. "With no allies, all Father could do was rigorously train us for when Matthew would return."

"What does he want?" Charlotte inquired breathlessly, shaken by Arick's revelation.

"All he said to Father all those years ago was that he would take what was his and join all of the realms." Arick sighed. "Whatever that means."

He still kept his eyes covered with his hands. No jokes. No foolery. Charlotte glanced at Atarah. Everyone did. They all held their breath. Arick had just confessed to being a halfling! Atarah's face was expressionless and her wings flared.

"Arick," she said softly. "Look at me."

Arick shook his head. "I can't"

"Yes, you can." Her voice turned stern.

Arick slowed, moved his hands away from his face, his gaze down. Slowly, he moved his eyes up. His eyes swam with emotions. Charlotte saw shame, anger, and fear.

"This is why you fainted earlier?" Atarah asked.

Arick nodded.

"Why?"

"Because I didn't want you to see me as a—"

"Demon?"

Arick flinched at the word, but nodded.

Atarah narrowed her eyes at him.

"You're a drama queen." Arick looked sharply at her.

"It is not funny, Atarah. I am a—" He couldn't finish the sentence, but the frustration in his eyes conveyed enough. Ben put a hand on Atarah's as if to pull her away from Arick, but she knocked his hand away.

"You are Arick," Atarah said sharply. Her tone was more commanding than before. Her wings flared. "You have a choice, and you have always chosen to be an annoying brother, loyal friend, and a great warrior. Nothing about who you are has changed. Why should that change who you are now?"

Arick looked shocked. "I am evil." He said it as if it should be obvious.

"So, you're evil because you think you're supposed to be evil? That you were made to be evil?" Atarah asked, her face twisted into a scowl. "This is annoying. Why would our parents keep something like this from us? You've been my dumbass of a brother my whole life, why does that change now?" Her hands slammed on the table in indignation.

Everyone looked at her shocked. Atarah was treading a dangerous line that went against what they had been raised to believe. Demons were evil and needed to be defeated, end of story. Arick was a demon. It should be a black and white case, but to her…

Charlotte glanced between Atarah and Arick a few times. She saw the sharp conviction in Atarah's eyes, while self-condemnation shrouded Arick's eyes. Arick regarded at Atarah in disbelief, then glanced at the table. To Charlotte's surprise,

Atarah was given support.

"Arick," Jared spoke up beside Ben. "We do not accept that you are evil."

"A drama queen, certainly," Brock jeered with sarcasm. "But no. Definitely not evil."

Galvin nodded in agreement with Brock and Jared. Gabriel and Ben stayed quiet, simply observing everyone, and gauging their reactions. Arick looked shocked, as if they had all lost their minds.

"Err—I don't know what to say—" Arick started, but was interrupted.

"Why don't you eat instead?" Luke said behind him, startling everyone. Luke appeared almost out of thin air, his expression easygoing. If Charlotte could guess, he'd probably heard everything.

"Come now." Luke frowned at their gawking faces. "You all need to eat because we are about to do something unconventional."

"Unconventional?" Charlotte nearly squeaked.

Luke smiled at her with excitement in his face.

"Why should we help you again?" Gabriel spoke up beside her. His voice was laced with suspicion.

Luke tilted his head to the side. "Do you not want to help, my decorations?"

Arick's lips twitched with amusement, but he kept silent.

"Well—" Gabriel sputtered. He glanced at Charlotte as if unsure.

After hearing everything with Arick and Atarah, Charlotte nodded.

"I guess... we do want to... help." Gabriel spoke.

Luke smiled nonetheless. "Excellent. Now eat up. For after this, you will all need to take our serum before we head out." He turned to leave, but Atarah called out another question.

"Where are we going?"

Luke paused and looked back at her.

"We are going to find the Watchers." With that, he turned away and walked toward another group of rangers.

A chill crept over Charlotte.

"Watchers," Ben hissed. His wings flared.

Everyone paled. Watchers were just as bad—or even worse—than demons. Watchers were criminals, angels that had gone through the realms and defied orders. Not only did they show themselves, but they also committed crimes in the human realm and even in the demon world. Many of the angels tried to escape their punishment and hide in the human realm. Some married, had families, and shared their spiritual powers with humans.

Growing up, the stories Charlotte had heard of the Watchers' offspring were terrifying. The offspring were called Nephilim, and were on the same level as demons, but stronger. They were large, bloodthirsty beasts that haunted the human realm for years. The destruction the offspring were capable of forced the hands of the Head Archangels. The Arch Heads deployed their armies to the human realm, starting the epic battle known as the Battle of the Nephilim. The Nephilim lost the battle; however, their parents slipped away. She shuddered. *Why in the realms are we going to see them? Where would you even find the Watchers?*

Gabriel shifted slightly closer to her. It looked as if he extended his wings to comfort her but thought better of it.

"Why does he seem to like you, Arick?" Atarah turned to face her brother. Arick shrugged as if he was just as confused as the rest of them.

"Are we…um, allowed to see the Watchers?" Jared glanced between everyone.

"I thought everyone was banned from being allowed to see them? Angels included," Brock chimed in.

Ben made the smallest cough Charlotte had ever heard, but it caught everyone's attention. They all turned to him. He blushed under all the scrutiny.

"Do you know something, Ben?" Atarah asked.

Ben's wings twitched before he relaxed under her gaze.

"From what I've learned about the Watchers, they were banned into an unseen space from the realms—an in-between place of our realms—cursed to wander aimlessly. They try to possess humans to feel some sort of form, or shelter, or place of belonging," he explained.

"Do humans let them do this?" Charlotte asked, slightly confused.

Ben glanced at her and shook his head. "From what I read, I think the human has to be in a specific mentality for the Watcher to possess them."

"All we know about the Watchers pertains to the Battle of the Nephilim," Arick murmured. He rubbed his chin as if he was trying to analyze something.

Brock scoffed. "We've all learned about that. The Watchers were banished by the Trinity."

"Yes, but there is more," Ben said gravely. He looked around at all of them. "The Watchers have a way to return either to our realm or the demon realm."

"What?" Atarah said as her eyes widened.

Everyone jaws dropped.

"How?" Charlotte chimed in.

Ben grimaced. "They can kinda hitchhike onto an angel or demon that enters into another realm. Or they can be redeemed in our world by a large act of compassion. With that act, they will be granted their own body. But, in the demon world, they cannot be redeemed. They will always have to possess a host body and will never feel at home."

"Why would they even bother trying to possess a demon's body, then?" Gabriel inquired.

Ben gave a small shrug. "I am sure they are just trying anything to escape the human realm. The ancient text said that to be without form is… very uncomfortable." He shuddered.

"To be like that for centuries and no end in sight... I can't imagine."

Silence followed. Everyone was lost in their own thoughts for a moment. The gravity of the situation crashed onto Charlotte once more. She glanced at Atarah, Arick, and Ben. Did she have the strength to keep up with them?

"All right, princes and princesses." A voice drew their attention from behind Ben. Flynn stood before them carrying bottles of a familiar-looking liquid. The serum. It was slightly darker than the one Charlotte had taken before.

"This is our version of the serum. It is more potent, so it will last longer than any other serum you have had before." Flynn passed one vial around for each of them.

Charlotte tried not to grimace as she took it.

"You can summon your wings, *but* be forewarned"—Flynn looked each of them in their eyes before finishing—"it will feel like your back is ripping apart."

Someone laughed behind Flynn. "Because it is ripping apart."

Charlotte saw Imani not far from where they sat. A knowing smirk was on her features.

Flynn's lips twitched as he held back his smile. He shook his head and turned back to them.

"This serum lasts for three to four months, instead of only several hours," Flynn explained. He glanced between Arick and everyone else, with a slight frown.

"Depending on your body size and amount of power you have, the effect may not last as long, so keep aware of any constant pain in your back. That may be the serum wearing off."

"Where do we get more once the serum runs out?" Arick turned the vial in his hand.

Charlotte looked down at her own vial, wondering what the components were that made the serum different from home.

"Any ranger you encounter will always have a few on them in case of emergencies," Flynn explained. "Ask any of them."

The vial was small. No bigger than her own pinkie finger. Very easy to travel with.

"Can we carry a few of our own? Instead of relying on other rangers for more," Charlotte asked softly.

Flynn glanced at her with a bemused expression. "You plan to be with us longer than three months, princess?"

Charlotte's face warmed under his teasing. She hesitantly shook her head, but she was not sure what she was going to do. Something must have shown in her face for Flynn softened slightly.

Flynn nodded toward their food. "You all really do need to eat. We have a long journey ahead of us." With that, Flynn turned around and walked back to Imani. All of her and Flynn's food was gone. Charlotte glanced down to see none of her group had touched their food. Her stomach was in so many knots, the thought of eating was difficult.

"He's right," Atarah said quietly. "We need to eat, and we need to eat fast. Everyone else is done and is waiting on us."

Charlotte shot her head up and glanced around. Atarah was right. Most of the other rangers were milling about while others gave them impatient glances. Charlotte turned back to her food and bit into her sandwich. She could barely taste any flavor, but she kept chewing anyway. Everyone devoured their food quickly and then drank the serum. Charlotte closed her eyes and quickly drained the serum. She braced herself for the sharp, bitter taste to fill her mouth and throat, but none came. Instead of bitterness, she tasted a strong aroma of spices—cinnamon and cardamom filled her mouth. A dull ache stretched throughout her back as her wings shifted. While the muscles of her back constricted, her wings folded into themselves, snapping a few tendons at a time.

Slowly, her wings disappeared into her back, giving her

enough time to adjust to the change in weight. Her powers slowly faded as if a light within her dimmed from the serum. She sat there feeling almost completely human. Or what she imagined a human felt like. She glanced around. Atarah's petite frame appeared smaller without her wings. Both Ben and Gabriel winced at the brief pain from the change, but otherwise looked almost bored. Charlotte marveled at how painless this serum was compared to the one they had back home.

A loud clap called everyone's attention to the front. Luke stood at center stage with his arms raised above his head.

"Time to head out!" he boomed with enthusiasm.

A cheer erupted and all of the rangers ran toward the lower left of the stage. They entered a dark tunnel that Charlotte had not noticed. Charlotte would have remained frozen if it had not been for Atarah jerking her into action.

"Let's not get left behind!" she yelled above the noise of the ranger's cheers.

With that, they all sprinted toward the rangers, following them into the dark abyss.

Chapter 7

The sun made its way toward the horizon, creating a vibrant red hue across the sky. Sand billowed about as the wind slashed through the dunes. Elijah adjusted his shemagh once more. He wished he could protect his eyes against the flickering sand but resisted. He was already struggling to keep up with Mikael's grueling pace. They had flown all day with almost no breaks or food. He silently prayed that Mikael would stop soon to eat. He dared a glance ahead to see Mikael powerfully flapping his wings in a tireless beat. He did not seem exhausted in the slightest. Elijah resisted a groan and flapped his wings faster. Mikael had gotten even further ahead, leaving him behind.

Still nowhere near the border, they would have to camp soon for the night. Elijah could see nothing but the golden sand for miles on end. As the sun passed the horizon, the color of the sky turned from a deep red to sherbet pink color. He glanced at the setting sun, thinking of his family. How he wished he could bring them all together once more. He thought back to the letters Noah had sent him from Mortem. Noah had shared all the knowledge he had gained from the libraries in Mortem and Quaesitor. Elijah had been shocked at how much Noah managed to learn in such a short amount of time. His son made him nervous when he mentioned reaching out to Seraphim instead of coming home. Before Elijah left his home, he franticly wrote back to Noah to never approach a

Seraphim, especially by himself. Elijah hoped his letter would reach his son in time, so he would not go snooping around deep in the caverns of Mortem.

Elijah shuddered.

"Elijah!" Mikael yelled from in front. He sped up so he could hear Mikael better.

"What is it?" Elijah shouted back, hating the sand that flew into his mouth as he spoke.

"I did not plan to camp for the night." Mikael turned to look at him briefly. "Do you think you can keep going throughout the night?"

Elijah spurted as his heart sank. He knew Michael angels were freaks of nature, but to this extent?!

Mikael must have seen the despair in his eyes, for he slowed down and descended without a word. Elijah gritted his teeth.

"We can keep going," he boomed down at Mikael.

Mikael shook his head. "We will stop here for a moment."

Elijah flew down and landed on the soft sand. They stood on the side of a large dune, which protected them from the flying sand. Relieved, he shook out his head, letting the sand rain down.

"I have a bad habit of pushing others until the point of breaking," Mikael spoke as he brushed the sand off. "I've been slowly learning over the years on how to pick up how others are *really* doing, despite the... discomfort." Mikael looked deep in thought. "It is one of the hardest things I've had to learn."

Elijah was unsure of what to say back to Mikael. All he could think to do was to open his pack and share his ration of food with Mikael. Mikael started to shake his head, but Elijah shoved the bread into his hand.

"It's important to pick up your body's discomfort too," Elijah insisted.

Mikael gave the smallest of grins and nodded thanks to

him.

They sat in silence while they ate. The sun had descended well past the horizon, allowing the dark sky to come forward. Stars began to twinkle in the distance to announce their arrival. Elijah thought about his family once more, wondering how they were doing. How was Charlotte while in the human world full of danger? How was Elizabeth? She had become so withdrawn after Charlotte went into the human world. It hurt him to leave her side. He wondered for what felt like the hundredth time how he could help his wife. She refused for any of their staff to help her. She was paranoid that someone was out to hurt her. Now that he was away, she must truly feel scared and alone. Elijah wanted to bury his head in the sand with shame. He knew he needed to help Mikael track down the Abaddon, but it still caused his heart to ache that he left Elizabeth, no matter how brief this trip could be.

He switched his thoughts to his son, Noah, wondering if he would venture into the underground labyrinth of Mortem—the labyrinth known as the Maze of Uncertainty. In the dark caverns of Mortem, past the Head Tree, laid tunnels that led to a variety of places. No angel, demon, or any spiritual entity had ever been able to map out the maze successfully. Despite the passionate efforts of numerous Raziel and Selaphiel angels exploring the cave, no one had prevailed. In fact, those who explored the cave were either never heard from again or came out a completely different person than before.

Elijah knew from his own exploration how the maze could change someone. He grimaced as he remembered his first encounter with a Seraphim. Back when he had thought Ava was taken by Mikael, he had sought out a Seraphim. Seraphim were ranked higher than Archangels and incredibly powerful. So strong that Elijah wanted to plead his case to one in hope of getting his daughter back. He knew he could never win a fight against Mikael. So, he thought surely a Seraphim could do the trick. He nearly laughed at his own foolishness.

The maze was so dark and devoid of light that there was no way to tell how much time had passed. He could have been down there for days for all he knew. With a small lantern to guide him, he searched in the maze. Seraphim were not the only ones in the labyrinth, so he had brought with him a variety of weapons in case he needed to fight. Many monsters lived in the caverns. Wyrms, j'ba fofis, cherufes, grootslangs, ahools, and olitiaus were only a few of the monsters a traveler needed to avoid. The maze was also dangerous because the terrain could change at any moment. It could be dark and damp in one area, but only a few steps away, one could suddenly be surrounded by rivers of lava or a beautiful oasis. One never knew what to expect while in the maze. The Maze of Uncertainty, indeed.

Luckily for him, he had stumbled upon a Seraphim early in his journey. He had climbed up a tall bed of rock, following a glow. Upon the top, Elijah saw a beautiful oasis filled with luscious, green plants and a stunning waterfall that sparkled. He had been so dazzled by the beauty of the land before him he had almost missed a female Seraphim lounging in a tree.

Seraphim were visually stunning creatures. Bearing three pairs of wings, they were often so fast, it was rumored the expression "death on swift wings" originated from the Seraphim. The Seraphim wore a silvery hood that covered most of her face, while the rest of her outfit was quite revealing. Her silvery tunic had slits up the sides of her thighs and a deep V-neck that nearly reached her stomach. She sat in a large tree wrapped in vines, watching him. Her top pair of wings hugged around her head, further concealing her face, while the bottom pair of wings covered her feet. The middle pair of wings hung causally by her side. The wings were so bright, Elijah thought they looked more like stars than wings. The power that radiated from her brought Elijah to his knees as soon as he looked upon her.

Such overwhelming strength, and she was not trying. She

regarded him for a moment as if his entrance brought her out of boredom. Elijah was so shaken by her presence he couldn't think of anything to say. His own wings trembled by his side. He gathered his courage as he remembered why he had ventured so far. Ava.

"I—" Elijah had struggled for words. He lifted his head to look at the Seraphim. Her hood was turned away, making it easier to look at her.

"*You've come here looking for power.*" Her voice was rich and vibrated with each word.

"I need help. Please, the Michael Clan has overstepped—"

She extended her middle wing and pointed it at him. "*You Archangels are children of the Trinity. Mere children.*"

Elijah could not see her eyes, but froze beneath her gaze, nonetheless.

"*We are not children of the Trinity. We are servants.*" She waved her wing out to the side. A strong wind knocked Elijah's bowed form back beyond the wall he had climbed. Back into the darkness of the maze.

"*Go back, child. Go back.*"

Her voice followed him all the way down until he hit the bottom. He had been so bewildered by her power, he couldn't move for a long while. Even the darkness of the maze hadn't scared him as much as she did. Like a mouse in the presence of a lion. He could do nothing but tremble and run away.

Elijah shook himself from the memory. The magnitude of her power from one wing swipe overtook him. Just one push. He shuddered at the thought of what would have happened if she had used all six of her wings. His encounter with the Seraphim had been merciful. She could have easily killed him for no other crime than speaking. The Seraphim were ranked so much higher than Archs; for him to speak to one was nearly insubordinate. He prayed and hoped Noah would not attempt to find one, like he had foolishly done.

"I don't wish for whatever memory came into your mind,

Elijah." Mikael's voice brought him back into the present.

"Nor do I wish for anyone to endure such a memory," Elijah spoke back. In hopes of chasing his own memory away, he asked, "Have you ever met a higher ranked angel? A Cherubim?"

The lines around Mikael's jaw grew taunt as if the memory was not a welcome one.

"Once," Mikael said softly. "It was the first time in my entire life that I felt small and helpless against an opponent."

"An opponent?" Elijah asked, shocked. "Did you foolishly try to challenge a Cherubim?"

Mikael chuckled a little. "You do stupid things when you are young." Mikael smiled slightly. "Matthew saved my ass by then. We nearly wet ourselves when the Cherubim transformed."

"What happened?" Elijah's curiosity got the better of him.

"Oh." Mikael sighed. "I was on a mission to prove to my father that I was strong. So, I thought challenging a Cherubim was a good way to prove it." Mikael rubbed the back of his neck and gave a humorless laugh. "I stumbled upon one and challenged it to a fight. The Cherubim appeared to be male, and it laughed at me. Like a cat amused by a bird's attempt to fight back. The Cherubim kicked my ass, and it wasn't taking our little 'fight'"—Mikael did air quotes—"seriously. If you could even call it a fight. It was mostly me getting knocked around, but I was too stubborn to yield." Mikael sighed again. "Then something changed. Something seemed to catch the Cherubim's attention. He looked south as if someone had called him. He then tried to fly away." Mikael winced. "I tried to stop him, and that was when he got irritated. The look in his eyes told me that play time was over. It got so silent and still, not even the wind dared to blow. I froze out of fear. Then he began to lift one of his wings, with real intent. Not the swatting around he had done earlier, but a real attack. Thankfully, Matthew had followed me there, worried about me. He darted through there, grabbed me by the collar, and dragged me out so fast I could do nothing but watch the Cherubim shrink in size as we retreated. He flew so fast away from the Cherubim; he didn't stop until we got back home to Sanctum." He gave a small grin.

"We were still afraid, even back at our home, far away from the creature. We shook with terror in our rooms. It wasn't until a while later that we began to laugh at what happened, from fear. Because at that moment, when the Cherubim looked at me with real intent to fight, I knew we had just escaped death." Mikael looked at him. "The Cherubim never dropped his wings, either. I could tell from the look of all his eyes, he was done 'playing.' He was no longer amused." Mikael scoffed. "We all do stupid things when we're young. It nearly killed me."

"Where was this? What did the Cherubim look like?" Elijah asked, fascinated.

Cherubim were ranked higher than Archs as well, but ranked lower than Seraphim. The ranking system of power was angels, principalities, Archangels, Cherubim, and then Seraphim. To challenge a Cherubim would have been a big deal.

"The Cherubim was on the border of Lanua and Belli Causa. It was by the flowering trees of Lanua when I discovered him. He had four wings that were red. His face—" Mikael hesitated.

"Yes?" Elijah was desperately curious. *Did he see the four heads?*

"It depended on what facet he chose. He changed his face often."

"It is said that when a Cherubim is in combat, he opens up all of his faces… and eyes. Is that what you meant when you said he shifted?" Elijah looked at Mikael for confirmation.

Mikael nodded. "He had dozens of eyes all over his body, his elbows, legs, and arms—everywhere. All with the same look of intent. They were closed until that last moment. The eyeballs opened up everywhere. The head of a lion and ox joined his regular head at the top, creating the most unnerving sight before me." Mikael shuddered. "The sight sometimes still haunts my dreams occasionally."

"Why was he there? I thought Cherubim preferred to stay on the southern islands off the Arena coast." Elijah couldn't help but look to the west.

Mikael shook his head. "I never knew why he was there. So far north. I didn't care enough to ask. I was too self-absorbed to notice." Mikael shrugged. "Maybe he was being called back to the island. Who knows?"

"You almost asked them for help?" Elijah remembered an earlier part of their conversation.

"Almost," Mikael said quietly.

"In case you run into Matthew?"

Mikael nodded. "I can handle the Abaddon, but I can't fight both Matthew and the Abaddon." Mikael peered up at the stars as he spoke.

"I have a difficult question for you, Mikael." Elijah stared up at the stars. He laid back against the sand dune, and exhaustion from the day settled in.

"Yes?" Mikael leaned back with his wings at ease. However, Elijah doubted that he was relaxed.

"Are you preparing to kill Matthew or are you trying to rescue him?" Elijah kept his gaze forward.

For a long moment, there was silence. Tension came back into his body as he waited for Mikael's reply. He needed to know Mikael's intention and resolve in case they did stumble upon Matthew. Elijah had no intention of saving the man who had caused his family so much harm.

Mikael released a long sigh before answering. "I am preparing myself for whatever may happen."

"That is not a direct answer."

"Life is not direct," Mikael retorted back. "Never would I

have thought that Matthew would have harmed others to such a degree. Nor that I, of all people, would end in the position I am in today."

"Your resolve sounds weak."

Mikael was silent for a moment.

"Things are not black and white," Mikael finally said. "A month ago, you had a strong resolve to try to take away everyone I love."

"That was different."

"If you keep the same mindset, you'll find yourself saying that quite often," Mikael said softly. "Through all of my mistakes, I am learning to... not jump to any conclusions quickly."

Silence followed once more. This time, the silence meant that it was time to rest for the night. Elijah glanced at Mikael once before looking back up at the starry sky. Mikael was not who Elijah had always thought him to be. He always thought of him as hotheaded, immature, and obnoxious when they were young Archs. He agreed with him that no one had foreseen him becoming the Head of the Michael Clan.

Many years ago, young Arch heirs often saw each other. When Elijah was growing up, many clans sent their heirs to other regions as a way to learn about each other. Elijah went to Belli Causa to learn how to fight. It had been his first time meeting Mikael and Matthew. They had been so young then. Yet, they had both towered over him in height. Elijah had thought they were generals. He had to remind himself several times that he was older than them to gather his confidence. He had been in his late teens, while Mikael had just turned thirteen years old, and Matthew was a couple years older.

While he thought they were adults upon first glance, only a few moments later would he realize his mistake. Mikael was so silly and rambunctious back in those days; Elijah thought he would be sent off to be a ranger. Matthew, in contrast, was a gentle giant, who seemed to have endless patience for his brother. They were both fearsome fighters, easily overpowering anyone in their class. However, Matthew always beat Mikael in fights. Mikael held a passionate, raw power and strength in fights. Matthew possessed more calculated power. Matthew was smart, tactical, and quiet with watchful eyes during the few days Elijah stayed with the Michael Arch family. They had spoken several times, mostly during fighting lessons. Matthew always carried himself so well that Elijah had looked forward to the day they were both Head Archs.

Elijah remembered when the news broke of Matthew's death. It had sent shock waves across all the regions. Matthew was known for being intelligent, strong, and an overall great heir to the Michael Clan. The memorial was a quiet, somber event by the Dark River at the border of Belli Causa. Everyone had worn blue to show respect to the Michael Clan. He remembered seeing Mikael off to the side and did a double take. Gone was the silly child. By then, they were both well into their adult years. Elijah had already married Elizabeth, who had just given birth to Charlotte a couple days earlier. He had insisted for her to stay home to recover from the birthing process while the rest of the family visited. Ava had been a young adolescent, standing by his side while he held little Noah at the funeral. Ava had been promised to Matthew for when she turned eighteen years old, which was only a few years away when he passed.

Mikael had stood at the edge of the forest as if he was watching the events of the funeral unfold, instead of being a part of it. His eyes still burned with a passionate fire from childhood, but there was more reservation within them. Mikael had matured, but there had been many painful lessons to go with his maturity. With his parents and brother gone, he had become Head Arch overnight and alone. That title looked heavy, even on him. Many people had gone up to him to offer their condolences, but he had stood there stoically. No—as if he was bracing for the painful impact each condolence would give.

Having lost his own parents, Elijah had looked on with sympathy then and did not approach him. Many Archs had low expectations for him as a leader, simply because he had paled in comparison. Matthew had been the kind, gentle, yet strong leader everyone had looked forward to. Matthew… the monster who had hurt his daughter. Elijah clenched his fists in anger. He could not foresee a future where he did not try to kill him.

Elijah came back to the present, away from his memories. He glanced at Mikael, who still looked up at the stars deep in thought.

"How is Ava?" Elijah asked gently.

The lines in Mikael's face noticeably softened at the mention of her name. He gave a small smile as if her very name gave him joy. "She is doing well. Scared for her family, but well."

"Will she—" Elijah hesitated. "Will she ever forgive us?"

Mikael scoffed. "She couldn't hold a grudge to save her life. Of course, she forgives you." Mikael paused. "However, she was still scared of what you would do if you found out about Arick."

At the mention of Arick, Elijah tensed. Matthew's son.

"*Our* son's safety was what kept us hidden away for so many years," Mikael said, pinning his eyes on Elijah. "I will not come between you and Ava ever again, Elijah, but know this."

Elijah watched Mikael's eyes. His golden eyes glowed against the night. Burning as they did before when he was young.

"You cannot accept Ava with open arms and push Arick away. She will not have it. Nor will Atarah. Nor will I," Mikael spoke firmly.

"Why do you all stand behind him so strongly? Does it not anger or upset you knowing what he is?" Elijah struggled to keep his disgust out of his voice.

"At first, it terrified me," Mikael answered. "I don't know why, but I almost expected a little demon monster to come out instead of him. As he grew up, I even tried to push him, to anger him during training to see if he would... snap. Or change into a demon. But he never did. No matter how much I pushed him." Mikael looked back at the sky. "We stand by him because we love him. It's as simple as that."

"Ava loves him?" he said it more as a question than a statement.

"Yes."

"Then... I will try too." Elijah sighed.

"One does not try love. You simply do."

Elijah let out a frustrated laugh. "All I want is my family back together, and yet, that seems impossible."

Mikael grunted as he shifted into a more comfortable position. "You embraced Atarah pretty quickly. Give Arick a chance, and you will embrace him too."

Elijah pondered this. Noah and Charlotte had been really taken with Atarah and Arick. Noah always had a hard time warming up to others, yet he accepted Arick. If his children could accept Arick, he would try. He gave out a long exhale and loosened tension throughout his body. Arick might be the key he needed to bring his family together. Elijah turned his body and closed his eyes. Dawn would approach too quickly when someone had a restless mind at night. Elijah quieted his mind and tried to drift asleep.

Ava stared out into the far distance of the mountains. Summer was not too far away, making the trek across the border easier. Even decades later, she still had a hard time traveling around Belli Causa and not getting lost. Dawn was about to break over the horizon, announcing the beginning of a new day. She gathered her courage, along with her things, as she broke down her camp.

"Would you like some help, my lady?" a gentle voice asked from behind.

Ava turned to see Atticus, Mikael's most loyal general. He had insisted on accompanying her on this journey. She smiled fondly, but shook her head. The task of breaking down the camp helped with her nervousness.

Atticus was indeed a great friend to have with her, making sure she crossed the land safely. She was scared but determined to reach Ventus to talk with her mother. While Mikael was with her father, she thought now was the best time to talk with her mother face-to-face. She loved Mikael and her father, but they were too protective and would want to moderate. She had not seen her mother since the disastrous summit meeting. She shook her head. *No, if my family can face dangers head on, so can I,* she thought.

After the battle with the Abaddon and learning how both of her children were in the human realm, Ava had to do something. Mikael was right. They had been holed up for too long. Ava's hands shook as she looked east. Fear gripped her as she thought of all the dangers that could occur beyond the border. Except for the summit meeting, this would be her first time leaving Belli Causa. Going to the human realm felt safer than crossing her childhood region's border.

"I will not let anything or anyone harm you," Atticus said firmly. He was watching her shaking hands closely.

Tears sprang to Ava's eyes, threatening to spill over. Atticus was there during those earlier days when Ava first arrived at Belli Causa. He knew how difficult this would be for her. She sniffled and tried to hold her tears back. *No, I can't live in fear,* she told herself.

"Thank you, Atticus." Her voice shook as she spoke.

She finished packing her few items and strapped down her pack. They were traveling light, with nothing more than a single pack for both of them. Atticus wore dozens of lethal weapons, while Ava carried one. An old, blue dagger that Mikael had made for her. The handle was made of dark wood from the trees in the region. The blade came from hard, blue ruby stone from the deep depths of the mountains. This was the first weapon Ava had ever been given. She cherished it now as some courage came to her. The dagger warmed against her thigh as if it sensed her resolve.

She put one foot in front of the other. Atticus followed in silent support. At first, he had been opposed to her leaving Sanctum, only because he thought Mikael should go with her to Ventus. Ava persisted anyway. Mikael, as sweet and tender as he was with her, would give her too much support. Too crowding. She needed to do this on her own. It would prove something to herself that she could do this alone.

They traveled for the next few hours in silence. Her shaking increased with each step, but she persisted. Her thoughts drifted to her children for more inspiration. Arick had the strength of a mountain that could withstand anything thrown at him, while Atarah's strength was more like a fire that could burn anything in sight. Her heart ached for them. She missed them terribly.

Their journey was uneventful, much to her relief. The trees started to thin out as they reached the edge of the border that led into Silva. Soon, the bright, green rolling hills appeared. After the hills would be the autumn leaves. Nostalgia filled Ava as she gazed upon her childhood home. Oh, how she had loved to play in the leaves when she was younger. She made dresses out of the leaves for fun in her youth. Her mother had taught her how to weave clothes and held fashion events for her.

Her mother... From what she had seen at the summit meeting, she had greatly changed. Her mother's eyes had sent chills through Ava. Her eyes had looked at her children with such distaste it had shaken her. Growing up, her mother had been carefree, kind, and open. At the meeting, she appeared withdrawn and hardened. When she was young, her mother had been like fresh river water, always easygoing. Now it was as if she were ice. Frigid. She wondered again how her mother would react when she saw her.

They paused as they reached the plain, grass field. The invisible border line was just before them. Atticus waited patiently as she took a couple of deep breaths. Her legs shook. Her eyes flitted about everywhere as if demons would pop out at any moment, ready to grab her when she crossed the border. No one was around them, though, not for miles. The openness scared her. Made her too exposed. Even years later, she was still afraid of *him*. The darkness of that night began to creep up on her. Memories suffocated her. Bruises throbbed under her skin, invisible to anyone but her. The memory of the pain from that night had mercifully lessened, but it never disappeared.

Her breathing became erratic. Muscles all across her body locked up as if Matthew was standing before her. Her wings flared as if she needed to fly away.

He is not here, she told her body. *He is not here. He is not here. He is not here. He is not here. He is not here.*

"Ava," Atticus said softly as if afraid of scaring her. "We can turn back."

That snapped Ava out of her frozen state. No, she did not want to turn back. She didn't want fear to dictate her life anymore. She took the single step needed to cross the border and stopped. She waited as the wind blew by.

Nothing happened.

She gazed around and saw no one. Just Atticus looking at her worriedly. She took another breath and another step. Then another and another. Atticus slowly followed her, his wings flared slightly as if he was ready to grab her and fly back to Sanctum.

No, she didn't want to go back. She wanted to travel into Silva and feel every step. With each step she took into the region, her shaking lessened. Breathing became easier. She no longer held it as if bracing for pain. The sun shined down on her, giving warmth. Her steps felt lighter as her fear slowly dissipated. She looked around and saw the land differently now. Instead of the openness feeling exposing, it was welcoming. Freeing. Her wings loosened and relaxed as she walked.

"Mikael would be so proud and happy for you," Atticus said.

Ava gave a breathless laugh as tears sprang to her eyes again. She did it. She crossed the border. She knew Mikael would be happy for her. She sniffled. She never thought she would feel safe away from Sanctum again, but this was a start.

"Thank you again for coming with me, Atticus. I couldn't have crossed without you," Ava said with a stronger voice.

Atticus shrugged. "You would have found a way over with or without me. But I am glad I came with you too." Atticus reached a hand out. "Let me grab your pack and we can fly the rest of the way."

Ava pondered for a moment before nodding and handing her pack over. The pack looked miniature on Atticus and would not hinder his flight at all. Ava tenderly opened her wings and lifted herself into the sky. Once in the air, Ava's heart bloomed with relief and joy. Her hands were steady. The tightness in her lungs loosened as she flew. The sun and wind blew across the field, and the trees were quickly approaching as if welcoming her return. Strength poured into her wings and body. For the first time in years, Ava was not afraid. The autumn trees swayed as they approached. Atticus was not far. He glided above her, ever watchful, staying alert for any dangers. She maneuvered low under the tree branches so the glow of the leaves could flutter around her.

A tenderness entered her heart as she looked around at the autumn forest. Slowly, the towns came into view. Raphael angels were out and about rebuilding structures that were destroyed by demons. Several paused in shock as they recognized her. She gave a small wave, unsure how the people would welcome her. A cheer erupted from the angels as they saw her fly by. Many screaming 'welcome home.' A few called out, happy that the 'lost princess' was home. The closer they got to Ventus, the more angels joined cheering her on. Tears flowed freely as she witnessed the citizens' welcome.

By the time she reached Ventus, she was a sobbing mess. She hadn't been home in so long. She did not deserve such a greeting. Her vision blurred from tears. She had to rely on Atticus to guide her around trees. The guidance mattered little because her body knew the way to her old home.

In the city, citizens threw golden leaves down from the treetops as a way of welcoming her home. She easily spotted the Head Tree and made a beeline for it, descending upon the large woodland steps leading to the mansion within the Head Tree. Vines and flowers around the Head Tree appeared to bloom upon her arrival. The large, russet pillars stood tall before her. She had made it back to her childhood home. The intercity guards looked upon her with surprise and then apprehension as they regarded Atticus. For his part, he tried to look as small and unthreatening as possible. Ava lifted her hand and flared her wings.

"It is all right," she said softly, relieved her voice was steady despite her crying. "He is with me."

The guards bowed deeply and relaxed their wings.

"Yes, m'lady," the guards said in unison.

She turned from them and made her way to the front door.

"I will wait out here if you need me, Ava," Atticus said.

Ava glanced back and gave him a nod. She hoped her gratitude was showing in her eyes because emotion gripped her throat strongly again. She took another deep breath and opened the door before her, taking a step inside the dark mansion.

Once the door closed behind her, Ava was covered in almost complete darkness. Fumbling around for a moment, she opened several windows to let the light in. The mansion was quiet and nearly devoid of life. *Odd,* she thought. While everything appeared structurally the same, there was a confined, nearly claustrophobic, atmosphere around the home. This was extremely unusual.

"Mother?" Ava called out.

She searched around and wondered where their staff were. She ventured deeper into the house, climbing the spiral staircase toward her parents' bedroom. The air felt stagnant as if no one had been living in the house. She walked slowly down the halls, looking at each picture with wistfulness. So many loving memories. She stared at a portrait with her mother and father holding onto each other, baby Charlotte in their arms, while she held onto her baby brother Noah. She looked so… different. The little girl in the picture felt like a stranger to her.

She continued, trying not to linger too long on any picture. Unease filled her heart at the silence in the house. She paused when she reached the bridge between the east and west wings. The children stayed in the east wing, while her parents stayed in the west wing. She ventured west. She came before the massive door of her parents' bedroom and knocked gently.

"Mother?" she called again softly. "It's me, Ava."

She cautiously pushed the door open. Now she was alarmed at her mother's silence. Once the door fully opened, she surveyed the bedroom. The bedroom was massive with a wide window in the far left corner. The enormous bed was composed of a wooden bed frame with pillars and a large, white comforter. The bed was made but empty. However, cuts and scratches marred the bedpost. Vines that normally wrapped around the bedpost were cut up and scattered along the bed as if someone had slashed it with a knife. Ava froze. Fear spread throughout her body, rooting her in place at the door. Her breathing stopped; her wings stiffened. She no longer felt attached to her body as fear consumed her. It was like she was watching herself stand there, struck with terror

A small sound caught her attention and shook her from her stupor. The concern for her mother quickly outgrew her hesitation. She took a step into the bedroom and walked carefully toward the bathroom on the right, where the noise came from. Beyond the bed, the room had two small green desks outlined with copper handles, side by side. A variety of plants and vines decorated the room. The green created a beautiful contrast to the surrounding wooden furniture, while colorful rugs spread across the room. She glanced back at the desks briefly. One being her father's desk, clean, orderly, and filled with pictures of his children, while the other—

Papers lay scattered across her mother's desk.. It was too far away for Ava to read; however, she could tell by the bold words that her writing was aggressive. She turned back to face the bathroom door. She quickly grabbed hold of the copper handle and opened the door before she lost her nerve.

"Ava?" a strange voice answered.

Ava stood rooted in place for a moment as her eyes adjusted. Her mother laid calmly in the freestanding, porcelain bathtub. The tub was by a large window looking out into dense woods. There was no water in the tub, nor was her mother gazing at her. Mother was staring out the window. Despite only seeing her profile, Ava could tell something was horribly off. Her mother's eyes were sunken in from lack of sleep. Ava used her powers to look at her through a healer's eyes. With the healer's eyes, she could see all ailments affecting a person. Her mother had not slept for some time. Her blood pressure was drastically low, while her heart rate was elevated. Her mother twitched as if sensing her gaze. She turned to face Ava, which gave her a better look.

Her mother's eyes were not right. There was redness where there should be white. Her pupils were constricted so much Ava could hardly see them. Veins were clearly visible all around her face, head, and neck. She suspected that if she looked under her clothes she would find the same. Her mother was not well. She sensed the simmering fear, anger, and agitation within her mother. This was not her usual behavior.

Mother regarded her for a moment. No real emotion was displayed on her face, except maybe an air of indifference. Ava's fear dissipated as she studied her, analyzing what was wrong. Her mother was sick, and she could help.

"What are you doing here?" Ava asked gently as her eyes traveled to her wings.

Feathers were wilting and falling off. Bald spots were evident along her mother's wings and hair. Her hair looked weak and thin. There was a shift in her eyes that caught Ava's attention. Ava racked her brain, trying to figure out what illness or disease her mother had. She walked into the bathroom and placed her hand gently on her mother's shoulder. At the touch, her mother had an explosive reaction. Mother went from a simmering calm to an aggressive anger.

Her mother hissed and whirled on her when she touched her shoulder. Her wings flared as mother swiped her—were those claws?—at Ava. She dodged her mother's attack, strangely unafraid. She did not fear her mother's unstable behavior, but she was concerned for her. Her mind analyzed her mother without horror or apprehension. Mother's hands were no longer hidden, showing blackened, sharp fingernails. Her eye color appeared redder, while her blood pressure and heart rate spiked high. Ava shifted her healing powers to her hands, knowing her new patient would not like what was to come next.

Her mother hissed again.

"Don't you dare touch me," she sneered.

Ava barely registered her words, but noted a difference in her voice. Raspier and deeper in tone. Another sign. Ava's power flowed through her like a cool river. Her energy moved from her to the environment, causing a faint blue glow around her. She was still not afraid. Not as another angry hiss came forward.

"You think I do not know what you are doing," the voice snarled.

"You know that I know you are not my mother," Ava replied calmly.

The demon—no, parasite—within her mother smiled cruelly at her. The demon crouched down, facing her as if ready to attack at any moment.

"You are the first to notice," the demon sneered.

"How long have you been hiding within my mother?" Ava tried to narrow down what kind of parasite this demon was.

It laughed at her, causing her mother's face to distort unnaturally.

"I was able to take root when you were taken," the demon bragged. "She was so distraught over your disappearance that none of those idiot Archs noticed. For years, I've been able to influence her." The demon smiled again, proud of it's accomplishment.

"But now her body is getting too hard to hide within for you?" Ava's eyes widened as she realized what kind of demon she was dealing with.

"It becomes too uncomfortable to stay hidden for so long." The demon scoffed. It looked at her with its intentions clear.

"You want to take root in my body now?" Ava replied. "That's what nybbas demons do. They're greedy and like to take control of their host's emotions."

Nybbas demons were known for their hunger and terror. They were a type of parasitic demon that took root within the brain, specifically within the region that controls emotion regulation and dreams. This demon looked and behaved quite similar to a leech once attached to a host's body. It latched onto that section of the brain and fed off any emotions of distress by causing nightmares. It also released toxins in the brain as a way to keep its host in a state of emotional distress.

Ava's heart ached. For her mother to have such a parasite unnoticed for so many years must have been agony and tortuous.

"Why wait so long?" Ava tried to stall as she thought of a plan. Nybbas demons usually moved on to a different host every few months. It was out of character for them to latch onto one for years.

"My orders were to keep this one under submission." It chuckled as if it knew she was stalling. Like a cat amused by a mouse's antics.

"Your orders?" Ava gasped.

"Yes. I was ordered to take out as many major healers as possible. This one." It moved its claw to point at her mother's face. "And then I was to go after the daughters." It smiled and crept forward. "Including you."

"Me?" Ava backed away. "What for?"

"I was supposed to take you last so that I can bring you to *him*." The demon shrugged. "But since you're here, I might as well latch onto you now."

That brought Ava's fear back. She didn't need to ask who 'him' was. Ava began to shake as she slowly realized the depth of Matthew's plans. Breathing was becoming hard as terror gripped its claws around her whole body. The demon chuckled as it watched her lock up.

"I thought there was going to be more of a fight from you." The demon moved from the tub and walked awkwardly toward her as if her mother's body was getting hard to control. It reached a hand toward her to grab hold of her neck, but stopped just inches away. A faint green glow returned to her mother's eyes. The redness lessened as the color returned, revealing her mother.

"Please." A faint whisper, but unmistakably her mother's real voice.

Her plea helped unlock Ava. She lifted her glowing hands on either side of her mother's neck. The redness to her eyes returned, and the demon hissed in anger. Her mother was using her power to fight against the demon. The demon snarled in a language Ava had never heard before. While she didn't understand what it was saying, she knew it was nothing good.

Ava created a small slit at the base of her mother's skull with her power. Both her body and her mother's started shaking for different reasons. Ava shook from fear and determination, while Elizabeth's body shook as the demon fought for control. She didn't have much time before the demon completely took over her mother again.

Ava flooded her power into her mother's head. Pushing away her fear, Ava thought of her family. She thought of all of the happiest moments in her life. Learning how to fly with her father. The time her mother taught her to sew. Playing with her baby brother and sister. The first time she held Arick in her arms. Teaching Atarah how to fly. The warmth and safety she felt whenever she was in Mikael's arms. She poured all of her love into her mother to drown out the parasite.

Screams erupted from both of them as they fought for control. A blue light glowed from Ava's powers as she pushed it forward. Elizabeth's eyes shined bright blue from the overflow of Ava's powers. The Head Tree beneath her fed into her, adding to her power. Ava didn't feel afraid. She felt strong. She pushed forward, taking a single step at a time until her mother's legs hit the tub once more. The power of the Head Tree and forest around her filled her up. With this newfound strength, she gave Elizabeth a final push and felt when the nybbas demon unlatched from her mother's head.

The demon washed out of her mother's head and plopped on the ground, squirming and squeaking in rage. Weakened, it was in a worm-like form, completely helpless without a host's body. It wiggled closer to Ava as if to latch onto her. Ava simply lifted her foot and stomped on it, killing it like she would any other bug.

A groan pulled Ava away from the crushed demon. Her mother laid slumped in the tub, shaking and weak.

"Mother?" Ava said frantically. "How do you feel?"

The grimace on her mother's face relaxed as her eyes focused on Ava. A weak smile played on her lips.

"That's my girl." Her soft, melodic voice had returned. The whites of her eyes were coming through, as well as the green color of her irises. The veins that had popped along her head slowly receded.

Ava sighed with relief. She put her arm under her mother's shoulders and helped her up and out of the bathtub. They slowly made their way toward the bed. They were both shaking badly. They ended up collapsing together on the floor, curling up toward one another.

That was how Atticus found her—curled up against her mother on the floor of the bedroom. He and several guards had burst through, alarmed by the light that had been shining out of the home.

Ava tried to speak to soothe Atticus's alarmed expression but couldn't. Her body was chilled and she was still shaking. She was vaguely aware that she was going into shock, but couldn't do anything about it.

"Send a messenger to Elijah and Mikael now!" Atticus shouted.

She wanted to protest, but the darkness of unconsciousness consumed her before she could even try. She fell into oblivion, still holding onto her mother's hand.

Chapter 8

A faint glow of bioluminescence followed along the cavern walls for what seemed like miles. Small crustaceans, barely visible to the eye, crawled everywhere and gave off a red light. The illumination gave the caves a disconcerting feel. Noah almost wished the small crustaceans were not around and that he could rely on his lantern. However, he knew it was foolish. Running into the bioluminescent crabs was pure luck, or at least that is what Zewal and Tariel had said a little while back. Noah cautiously looked back at his two companions to see how they fared. What he saw made the hairs on his neck stand up. Their faces looked purely ghoulish under the glowing red light, surrounded by the labyrinth's darkness. Their tall, lanky forms, along with their slow movements, simply looked creepy. Noah shuddered.

"We... are trying our… best here." Zewal tried to glare at Noah as he panted, but it came out as a grimace.

They looked like zombies, and that was putting it politely. Both of them took in deep breaths, neither of them used to prolonged exercise.

After Tariel had shown him the Head Tree, he insisted upon going into the Maze of Uncertainty. He had read about the Seraphim and wanted to seek them out. He had many questions that he thought they could answer. Tariel, concerned for him, told him not to go into the maze without talking to Zewal or Sewall. They happened to run into Zewal first. Upon explaining his plan, Zewal insisted that he wanted to accompany him into the labyrinth. Apparently, he wanted to ask the Seraphim some questions too. Tariel insisted on coming as well, despite her brother's protest, explaining she needed some answers. She stated that the book Noah had given her to decipher might help them in the maze.

Zewal had spent the next day preparing everything they would need for the dangerous trek. Noah knew there were monsters in the labyrinth, but the full scope of the danger didn't hit him until they became surrounded by darkness. The maze was so dark that Noah couldn't see his own hands. He had never been afraid of the dark, but the labyrinth was eerie—darkness so stifling it was oppressive and harsh—like a predator watching them come into its den, waiting for them to lower their guard. Noah kept his hand on the handle of his sword until they came across the crabs. Even with the little light the crabs provided, Noah's unease didn't lessen.

He knew there were many dangers in the maze and didn't want to end up as something's lunch. He glanced again at Zewal and Tariel. They leaned against the walls of the cave, trying to get their breath. Noah almost felt bad for setting a fast pace, but the maze was not a place to linger in.

"Can you see anything up ahead?" Noah asked Zewal and Tariel.

An advantage of Azrael angels being active at night was their excellent night vision. This crucial fact had not been lost upon Noah. They both helped prevent him from running into different rock structures. Noah was glad that they both had insisted upon coming.

Zewal gazed ahead at their path. His breathing seemed to finally calm down, but he winced as he looked at the path in front of them.

"The path gets steeper," Zewal said, standing up. "We will have to start climbing soon."

"This is a good thing, right?"

Zewal shook his head, but it was his sister who spoke.

"Usually, the steeper path means deadlier monsters up ahead," Tariel explained. "The larger monsters usually like to reside somewhere high so they can ambush prey."

"Oh…" Noah suppressed a groan. "Lovely." He withdrew his long dagger and turned to head up the path he couldn't see.

Zewal gave a harsh laugh and stopped him.

"Why must you be so reckless?" Zewal chided him. "Since this path could be more dangerous, let me lead the way this time. I'll see any signs of danger much faster than you will."

"Zewal is right," Tariel chimed in. "Now is not the time to rush into something headfirst."

Noah sighed and looked at them. He knew they were right, but he couldn't shake this jittery feeling. He gave a nod and Zewal made his way to the front of their path, drawing out his own dagger. Zewal made slow progress up the path, which made Noah grind his teeth in frustration. Nonetheless, he kept silent, knowing that asking him to go faster would be stupid.

All too soon, the steps they took became steep. So arduous that Noah had to put his dagger up to use his hands. They climbed up the wall with no clear path, other than the red, glowing light emanating from the crabs still around them. The microscopic crabs scuttled along the wall they climbed, causing Noah's hand to glow red after a few minutes. Tariel had said earlier that the crabs were harmless, but he didn't like the idea of anything crawling on his skin. They ascended up just as slowly as they had walked. Noah's muscles ached and burned as the climb progressed. The air became more stagant as they climbed, while dust descended on them mercilessly.

Noah gagged and coughed every so often, trying to clear his throat, but to no avail. He tried to grab his canteen once and nearly fell off the wall. He gripped the rocks so hard that he wondered if he would accidentally break his fingers. While he struggled, Zewal and Tariel took to rock climbing fairly well. They scaled the walls like lizards. Their pitch-dark eyes scanned the area around them with every step they took. The slow pace appeared to agree with them.

They trudged upward, pausing every few moments to look around for danger. The red lights of the crabs faded away the higher they climbed. Soon, they were encased in pure darkness once more. Noah froze. He couldn't reach the lantern hooked on his small pack. All of his limbs were clutching the rock wall, keeping him from falling. He couldn't even see where his hands and feet were. He flared his wings in fear and uncertainty. Maybe he could fly the rest of the way?

A cool hand came upon his leg, causing the hairs on his arm to stand up. Startled, he nearly lost his grip on the wall.

"It's me, Noah," Tariel's voice came in a harsh whisper.

Some of his muscles relaxed. With absolutely no sight and stuck climbing a wall, Noah felt quite helpless.

"Do not try to fly up," she whispered again. "The way up is very narrow, and the rocks are sharp. You will tear up your wings."

"Why are you whispering?" Noah whispered back.

"Because there is a j'ba fofi resting to our right," Zewal whispered from above.

Noah froze.

A gigantic spider was resting near them! J'ba fofi were large monsters that fed off anything wandering in the labyrinth. The eight long, thick legs they possessed were barbed and poisonous. Their bodies could grow larger than Michael angels. Noah wanted to throw up.

"We will be fine, Noah," Tariel said quietly. "Step where I say to step, and we should be able to pass by without waking it."

"Should?" Noah scoffed as quietly as he could. His arms began to shake. He wanted so badly to draw his dagger again, but couldn't risk it.

"Move your left foot up and left hand over your head a

little," Tariel directed quietly.

Noah had some difficulty moving his limbs because he wasn't sure where anything was in the dark space. The darkness consumed of all light; the only thing he was certain of was the rock he felt.

Their progress was slower as Tariel directed his every move. Noah's heart pounded in his ears so loudly that he was surprised the j'ba fofi didn't wake. He tried to keep his breathing quiet as he moved. His throat burned with the urge to cough, but he didn't dare. He couldn't hear any step or sound Zewal made, but knew he wasn't far away. Noah had no clue how much progress he was making or how close the j'ba fofi was. Time passed by like their agonizing climb. Painfully slowly.

As time passed, and Zewal's voice joined Tariel's in directing him.

"We are almost there, Noah. Just a little more up ahead."

"How much farther?" Noah asked desperately.

"Only a few more meters and the—"

Zewal's voice cut off as Noah's foot slipped. Suddenly, Noah was falling. In complete darkness, Noah flailed about, trying to grip onto something. Rocks cut his wings, shoulders, and back, and he struggled to regain his footing. He cried out in fear, and he waved his arms in front of him, trying to grab onto the rock wall. Hands grabbed Noah and slammed him back onto what Noah could only discern as the rock wall. Once on the wall, they all painfully froze as they listened to the rocks loudly crash down the walls of the cave.

Silence. Then a frightening hiss came from below.

The j'ba fofi was awake.

"Climb!" Zewal roared from above.

Blindly, Noah scurried as fast as he could in what he thought was an upward direction. He must have been right because Tariel nudged him anytime he veered in a different direction. The sharp rocks cut deep into Noah's hand, but he didn't dare slow down. His body tried to heal itself quickly, but that didn't stop his blood from seeping down his arms and legs. He could hear the j'ba fofi closing in on him as if it could smell his blood. Its legs clasped onto the rock like the sound of metal scraping across metal. The sound spurred him on to climb faster.

As fast as he could climb, Noah was not fast enough. Something pierced into his leg, cutting through muscle and bone. Noah cried out in pain and tried to get away, but was trapped. His left leg was broken and pinned to the wall by whatever had pierced him. A liquid dripped onto his neck and the spider's breath fell upon him. Noah gagged as the aroma of rotting flesh drifted over him.

Just as he thought this would be his death, the spider reared off of him and screeched in pain.

"GO!" Zewal boomed.

Noah crawled up using his arms the best he could, while his body tried to quickly heal itself. Times like this made Noah grateful he had been born a Raphael angel, immune to poisons. The j'ba fofi hissed weakly as they climbed. He could hear its body slowing down as they climbed higher. Noah wondered if Zewal and Tariel were using their powers to weaken the creature. *Hopefully to the point of near death,* Noah thought vehemently. Noah's bone snapped as it reset back into place, and he grunted in pain. It must have been one of the spider's legs that stabbed Noah, for the poison burned and inflamed his leg. After a moment, the cooling effect of his healing power lessened the pain. Noah sighed in relief that the spider came after him and not Zewal or Tariel.

They climbed up the wall as fast as they could, until finally Noah saw a light up ahead. They clawed their way toward it desperately. The j'ba fofi was only weakened, not completely out of the picture. It hissed from down below. They finally made it to the top of the wall and climbed out of the enclosed cavern.

"Quick, block it!" Zewal yelled.

They shoved whatever rocks were nearby into the thin slit of a hole they crawled out of. It took Noah a moment or two to realize a few things. First, the rocks they were grabbing were glowing crystals. Bright bluish green emanated from the crystals, creating a mesmerizing effect. Secondly, the spider would not follow them because the j'ba fofi did not like light. He sighed in relief and slumped down.

"Hey, it's all right now," Noah said, trying to catch his breath. He stretched his leg, aching and sore from healing.

Tariel and Zewal looked at him and then back at the dark cavern. Hesitant.

"The monster won't follow us with these glowing crystals," Noah explained.

Zewal and Tariel slumped alongside him, panting and exhausted. Noah could see the cuts and bruises on him healing. He turned to assess the damage on Zewal and Tariel.

"How are both of you doing?" Noah asked. His eyes slowly adjusted to the light.

"Just peachy," Zewal grunted.

Tariel rolled her black eyes at his response. "Zewal's wings were scratched by the cavern walls when he jumped on the j'ba fofi. Can you heal him?"

Noah nodded. He hadn't known Zewal had attacked the monster, effectively saving his life.

"Thank you, Zewal. Without that attack, I would have been spider food," Noah said sincerely.

He shifted to lift his hand toward Zewal's wings. After getting a good look at them, Noah realized Zewal's wings had taken some damage. Cuts and bruises painted across nearly his whole back. His pale, featherless wings twitched when Noah first touched them, but relaxed when his power began to seep into them.

"Thank you both for coming with me." He focused on transferring his healing energy to Zewal's wings. He was not as good of a healer as the rest of his family, but he could at least help with minor stuff.

Zewal scoffed, but Tariel responded to him.

"I am glad we came as well," Tariel replied.

She appeared to be in good shape. Paler than usual, but no injuries.

"All done," Noah said.

Zewal moved his wings cautiously. "You can lead the way now, Noah."

Noah chuckled. "I am not as eager as I once was." Noah looked at Tariel. "How about ladies first, Tariel?" He stood and beckoned her forward.

Tariel rolled her eyes, but grinned nonetheless. "Unlike either of you, I can lead despite the fear."

Zewal and Noah laughed nervously and didn't contradict her. They took in their surroundings for a moment. They were in a large open space surrounded by crystals, all varying in sizes. Some of the blue-green crystals were small, while others were taller than them. They all glowed, giving the space a decent amount of light. There were no monsters in sight, but something caught Noah's attention.

"Wait, listen," Noah whispered.

A trickling sound caught their attention. They wandered toward the sound, moving around large crystal structures as quietly as they could. Noah didn't want to stumble upon another sleeping monster. The crystals were so large that they provided great coverage. However, due to their glow, it took a moment for his eyes to adjust.

A small river nearly blended in with the cavern. The movement of the water caught Noah's eyes. The river moved downstream and into the pit they had just come from. He looked to where the river was flowing and could not see the end. His throat tightened in anticipation; he was extremely parched. The dust from the climb had nearly clogged his throat. Noah knelt toward the river and grabbed his canteen.

"Wait," Zewal said harshly. "This water might not be drinkable."

"Let me try it first," Noah said. "I will be able to tell if it is drinkable."

"How?" Tariel glanced at the water. Her nose was scrunched up as if disgusted by the idea of drinking it.

"If anything is poisonous or lethal, my body will be able to heal itself, and I can recover."

"Won't that be painful for you?" Tariel turned her glance to him.

"No more painful than a spider stabbing through my leg," Noah said dryly.

Zewal looked at the flowing water and then at Noah as if he was insane.

"It is your body. Go and try to kill yourself... I guess." Zewal frowned, watching him.

Noah scooped up a large amount into his canteen and quickly drank the water. The water was surprisingly warm and tasted minerally in flavor. After so much dust and rocks had descended upon them, the water felt amazing. His throat had been as dry as a desert after the climb.

After taking several large gulps, Noah waited. No burning sensation occurred, nor did his healing energy activate. Zewal and Tariel exchanged concerned looks while they waited in silence to see if he would begin to wither in pain. More minutes passed and Noah felt nothing. Noah glanced at Zewal.

"We will wait a little longer before drinking the river, just in case. We can load up our canteens and start walking while we wait." Zewal's black eyes scanned the area.

Tariel nodded.

"I think it is wise to keep moving," Noah said, looking upstream.

"We should follow the water. It will be the most likely path to lead up to the Seraphim." Tariel filled up her canteen.

"It will also be the path most teeming with… life." Zewal

scowled at the river as if it offended him.

"It is a risk we will have to take," Noah defended Tariel's plan. "It is the only lead we have, and provides a water source, which is rare in the labyrinth."

Zewal pursed his lips in displeasure, but didn't argue against them. Instead, he silently filled his canteen. Once they filled up on water, they continued on their path, traveling as silently as possible.

Noah set a fast pace, once again taking the lead. While Noah was swift, Tariel and Zewal were quieter on their feet. They made no noise or complaint; however, Noah knew the pace would tire them out quickly. He slowed down.

Noah glanced upward to see if they could maneuver around the cavern through flight. It was possible, but it would be cramped. The ceiling of the cave was tall but covered in large crystals, creating a spike-like appearance above. They wouldn't be able to fly very high or expand their wings all the way in some areas. The size of the crystals changed throughout their path, narrowing the opening ahead. Noah sighed. No, flying would be more of an inconvenience.

They continued onward in silence, with everyone in their own thoughts. Noah thought about his questions for when they did eventually come across the Seraphim. His thoughts traveled to what encountering the Seraphim might be like. Based on what he read prior to Tariel showing him the Head Tree, which was the starting point of the maze, Noah knew a bit. He understood there were monsters in the labyrinth and the Seraphim, but he did not know many details, other than that they existed. Every account on the Seraphim had been written in terror and awe of the six-winged creatures. They were older than the Original Archangels. A spiritual race filled with knowledge and enormous amounts of power. One of their powers was that they had the ability to change any form of matter!

With such power and knowledge, the text warned anyone

reading not to seek out the Seraphim. There was no explanation on why angels should avoid the Seraphim, just strict and fervent pleas not to pursue them. The texts they had on the Seraphim were ancient, and due to such little contact with the Seraphim, no one could confirm all of their powers. Maybe only a dozen or so angels had ever made contact with a Seraphim. Much of their written encounters were described in shock, horror, and panic. Noah hoped that with their vast knowledge, they could give some answers to help Arick. They might have some information that could help stop the demons coming into their world once and for all.

Noah clenched his fists in determination. He was more scared of facing a Seraphim than any other monster that might be in the labyrinth. For good reason. He would be foolish if he did not fear them, but he couldn't let that stop him.

A shudder shook the cavern walls, causing all the crystals to shimmer and sway dangerously above them, presenting more like sharp daggers dangling above their heads. *Another shudder like that and we could end up speared,* Noah thought.

Zewal scowled at the ceiling, while Tariel's eyes were ahead.

"There is something up there," Tariel whispered.

Noah drew his favored dagger and an axe. This time, he would be ready for an attack. Zewal and Tariel drew their weapons, consisting of two thin, curved swords. They slowly crept forward, using the larger crystals as cover. Another shudder vibrated through the enclosed cavern. The crystals shook dangerously loose above their heads. They couldn't stay here for long. Noah scaled up a crystal as quickly and quietly as he could for a better view.

Once at the top, Noah looked around and froze in fear. Not too far away, coiled around one of the large crystals was a grootslang. The serpent-like beast had four long tusks protruding from its mouth with a large, thick, broad head. Two huge ears flared out, making its head appear even larger. It was almost as if an elephant and snake had come together to create this terrifying creature. The scaly body coiled itself around a large crystal, tightening until the crystal began to crack. The grootslang then rammed its head into the crystal, causing it to shatter everywhere.

Many large cave bats scattered in different directions. The cave bats had been hiding behind the crystal that the grootslang destroyed. With incredible speed, the grootslang snapped its jaws around the fleeing bats. Dozens of sharp rows of teeth lined its mouth, trapping all that were too close. The screams of the bats filled the cave as the grootslang ate. They would have to pass this dangerous beast without getting spotted.

Noah opened his wings slightly and glided down to the ground. Zewal and Tariel looked at him expectantly.

"A grootslang is up ahead," Noah whispered.

Zewal hissed in displeasure.

"We can't seem to get a break." Tariel groaned.

Zewal shushed her. "Keep as quiet as possible. Grootslangs have excellent hearing. We won't be able to sneak past this monster."

"Well, what do you suggest?" Tariel whispered back.

Noah's wings twitched as he got an idea. He glanced at the flowing river, then back at Zewal and Tariel.

"We can use the river," Noah whispered. "I haven't felt any burning or pain since drinking it. So, I think it is safe for us to use."

Zewal frowned, but nodded. "grootslangs' eyesight is poor. The movement and sound of the water will help conceal us." Tariel's wings shook in fear.

"How do we know the water is harmless? Just because it didn't hurt a Raphael angel doesn't mean it won't hurt us." Tariel's voice quivered.

Tariel's hesitance sounded strange to Noah, but they didn't have time. Going into the water was their best option. The cries of the bats were starting to die down, literally. Once the bats were gone, the grootslang would be able to hear them and hunt them down.

"Take the leap of faith, Tariel," Noah whispered. "Because we don't have much time."

Tariel glanced between him and Zewal. Her expressionless black eyes rested on Zewal for a moment. Zewal placed a hand on her shoulder in silent support. Something must have passed between her and Zewal, for she nodded.

"All right."

With that, they moved stealthily into the water. They put their weapons up and carefully entered the river. The current was not too strong, nor was the river too deep. Noah got onto all fours, submerging his body. Only his head broke through the surface of the water. His hands gripped the larger rocks at the bottom of the river, while he kicked his legs against the current. Zewal and Tariel were not far behind him.

Noah understood Tariel's apprehension now.

She was not a confident swimmer.

Zewal opened his wing and waded into the water behind her. Zewal would be there to catch her easily if she slipped and flowed downstream. Crouching low in the river, they began to crawl upstream just as silence engulfed the cave. The bats were all gone, eaten by the grootslang. Carefully, keeping their heads barely above the water, they trudged forward.

Soon, they passed a river bend that brought them into full view of the grootslang. It sat coiled around itself, its pale eyes staring ahead blankly at the crystals. Its enormous ears were larger than its head, and they flared open wide, listening for any new movement. The river had been a wise choice. Upon a closer look, Noah could see an elongated nose that had sharp rows of teeth upon it too. It possessed small arms with claws, but most of its body looked like a snake. Scales covered the body nearly everywhere, except for the ears. The head was broad and thick with two small, pale eyes. It was truly a terrifying creature.

Not wanting to linger, Noah moved upstream. Tariel followed behind him. Her movements were jerky as she struggled to get the hang of swimming. Mercifully, the sound of the river covered her louder movements. Zewal drifted not far behind her, keeping his eyes on the grootslang. Noah tread slowly, feeling the way for Tariel. He indicated several times what rock to grab onto and pull from. However, their luck ran out when, suddenly, Noah felt a drop off.

The temperature of the water changed from warm to a deep, deep cold. The depth of the river changed drastically. It was no longer shallow with rocks to grab onto, but a bottomless floor. The river also widened before them, putting them no longer along the edge of the water, but now in the center of the river. A river with a stronger current too. They would have to really swim instead of crawling. Noah could see the barely contained panic in Tariel's face. Her wings were flared, and her arms and legs shook.

Noah silently cursed. If Tariel splashed around too much while swimming, the grootslang might hear them. Noah came alongside Tariel and opened his wings. Using his wings and the muscles of his back, he slightly lifted Tariel. Zewal caught onto Noah's plan and went to the opposite side. Now they both used their wings to carry Tariel, giving her enough support to stay afloat. She used her legs and wings to move upstream.

Noah groaned as he strained to keep her up, while swimming. Zewal grunted in effort, but they were almost around another river bend. They just needed to get far enough away from the grootslang. Come on, Noah thought. His back muscles burned against the strain on his wings. Tariel could probably sense their effort because she picked up the speed.

The grootslang still sat coiled around itself, staring ahead. It hadn't noticed them. Noah looked further upstream. They were so close to the riverbend.

Just a little farther. Noah strained.

They were beginning to swim around the river bend when

their wings gave out. Tariel dropped in the water and came back up sputtering and splashing. She tried to right herself and stay afloat. Zewal assisted his sister, but Noah immediately turned to look at the grootslang.

The grootslang's ears perked up in their direction. Slowly, its head turned toward them. Its tongue came out as if it was sniffing the air. It knew something was up. Tariel was still trying to swim upstream with Zewal pushing her along. The more she splashed, the more curious the grootslang seemed. It leisurely uncoiled its body and slithered to the water's edge.

Noah made up the rear as Zewal struggled to get his sister further away. Noah drew his dagger from his belt. The grootslang poked out its tongue again, and its ears twitched in different directions as if trying to pinpoint them. With the stronger current, the rushing water still gave them some coverage, while making it harder for them to get away.

"Noah!" Zewal hissed.

His voice was low, but Noah could hear him nonetheless. Noah turned back to face them. They had made it around the riverbend and were waiting for him. He put his dagger back in its holster and swam fast. Using all of his appendages, he swam around the riverbend just as the grootslang turned its head toward them.

Once the grootslang was out of sight, it was an all-out dash. They all kicked and flailed, trying to get even further upstream. The water was still deep, so they could not use anything as leverage. Worse still, the more upstream they went, the stronger the current became. Noah looked around and noticed fewer crystals around them. Fewer crystals meant less light. Noah looked back, and he could barely make out Tariel's face.

"We need to get out of the river." Tariel coughed. She struggled to stay above water.

"There!" Zewal called out.

Off to the side, Noah could make out a little bit of a shore.

They went for it. Zewal and Noah took turns pushing Tariel closer to shore. His whole body ached with the need to rest, but he continued forward. The dim lighting made him more fearful. He at least wanted to be on land if he couldn't see.

After what felt like miles, they finally collapsed on the shore. They all gasped for air. Wet, cold, and exhausted, Noah was truly starting to regret coming into the labyrinth.

"I think we lost it," Zewal said breathlessly.

"Next time, let's try flying around it." Tariel coughed.

Noah gave a humorless chuckle. If he had known that the river would have opened up wide, like it did, he would have flown in a heartbeat.

"Is everyone all right?" Noah asked, finally catching his breath.

Tariel struggled to stay upright, while Zewal groaned. Their wings slumped at the same time.

"I'll take that as a yes," Noah murmured. He sat up so he could properly inspect their surroundings. The river before them was wider and stronger. The ceiling appeared higher than before.

The crystals that dangled from the ceiling of the cave were in a large cluster. The blue light shining off of them gave an iridescent yet eerie glow to the labyrinth. The shore around them was small and surrounded by cave walls. The space was mostly taken up by the river. Only a few spots off to the side of the river gave him any solace. Noah tried to map out how they could swim from spot to spot, but another river bend, upstream, limited his view. Noah glanced between Tariel and Zewal. They both appeared to have the same idea as him. They looked at the river before them in dismay. Tariel grimaced as she regarded the closest 'shore' up ahead.

The term shore was pushing it. It really looked like enough clusters of rocks for them to grab onto to rest. They would have to do it. They could only keep moving ahead at this point or face the grootslang.

If only we had that oversized bat with us! Noah groaned inwardly. *We could definitely have taken on the grootslang.*

"We have no other choice." Zewal frowned and shifted his gaze to his sister. "Can you handle it?"

Tariel's usually pale face looked more strained, but she nodded.

"Do either of you know of any monsters that like water in the labyrinth?" Tariel asked, her eyes never leaving the water.

Noah shook his head, while Zewal seemed hesitant to answer. They all turned to the flowing river that once was their blessing, and now their challenge.

Noah trembled as he realized how much he was going to need Zewal and Tariel's help. For the first time, he wondered if they could make it out of the Maze of Uncertainty alive.

Chapter 9

Mikael removed his shawl from his head as he landed. The faint sounds of exhausted flaps told him Elijah was not far away. They had been traveling since the break of dawn. Following the Dark River all the way to the Coal Mountains in Joshua's region, Mikael pushed just outside of the cavern.

Tucked away between the mountains, the Dark River flowed down a large cavern, deep underneath the ground. Mikael grimaced. He did not want to follow the Abaddon underground and put themselves at a disadvantage. However, he suspected the Abaddon was trying to reach the Maze of Uncertainty.

Mikael cursed softly. The maze was the perfect place for the demon to hide, yet the worst place for them to fight it. He turned to a panting Elijah and waited for him to catch his breath.

"Have some bad news," Mikael huffed. "The Abaddon dove into the caverns below the Coal Mountains. It's heading to the Maze."

Elijah frowned. He moved to wipe the sweat off his brow as he responded.

"It went down there to hide most likely."

"Unless"—Mikael pondered—"Joshua told me of the possibility that somewhere in the Maze lies a portal leading to the demon realm."

"An open portal within the Maze of Uncertainty?" Elijah

asked incredulously. "Why not mention anything before?"

"Like all things about this cave, no one was certain it was true," Mikael responded gravely. "Joshua suspected another portal was open within the Coal Mountains, but he was never sure where. He only guessed one was open because of the vast number of demons that attacked his region."

"Mikael," Elijah said harshly. "My son may be down there."

He jerked his head to Elijah. "Are you sure?"

Elijah ran a hand through his sweat-coated curls. "No."

"Our children will be the death of us," Mikael whispered.

"What was that?" Elijah asked as he peered down the hole the river flowed.

"Nothing," he replied. "Come on. If he's down there or not, we need to neutralize that Abaddon."

Mikael tucked his wings tight to his sides as he dove down the large opening. He heard Elijah cursing behind him before the sound of falling water took over. Very quickly, he was encased in darkness. The sound of rushing water was his only clue on his surroundings. He opened his wings to slow his descent as the noise increased. The louder the noise, the closer he must be to the bottom.

He flapped his wings when his feet came into contact with water. Hovering just above the water's surface, he tested its depth. Cautiously lowering his body into the water, he stretched out his hands and feet. Nothing but warm river water greeted him. Once he was about chest deep, he gave up. He lifted himself back out of the water before his wings could get wet. Slowly, his eyes adjusted to the dark maze. Small, blue glowing crystals lined the walls of the Maze's entrance. He barely made out the ripples in the water as it flowed further downstream.

"Mikael!" Elijah whispered harshly above him. "Where the hell are you? I can't see a damn thing."

"Right above you," he said. "Careful, let your eyes adjust.

I am just above the water, and it goes down deep."

"Adjust?"

"There are faint blue crystals glowing along the river's edge. It is not much, but there is some light."

"Ah!" Elijah yelled as he fell into the river. His wings flapped loudly as he struggled to get back up in the air.

"Here!" Mikael grabbed ahold of Elijah's shirt. He gave a strong flap upward and lifted Elijah out of the water.

"Be more careful," Mikael barked. "There are dangerous demons that thrive in the water."

"You don't have to tell me twice," Elijah groaned. "I've been down here before, and I never wanted to come back."

"Come on," Mikael urged. "Try not to disturb the water."

They traveled downstream, hovering just above the water. As they flew, the crystals grew in size, and created more light. Mikael moved with caution. He'd studied all the stories about this maze. He knew of the monsters that dwelled down here.

The river narrowed and widened in various spots through the tunnel, but never opened up enough space to land. The crystals multiplied in number the further down they went. The dark blue, iridescent color glistened against the cave walls. He maneuvered low to avoid a dropped ceiling as the sounds of the river picked up. A waterfall roared just ahead of them.

Mikael turned to check on Elijah, who gave a reluctant nod.

"Something tells me trouble is that way," Elijah said grimly.

Mikael led the way. As he flew, the river changed terrain. More rocks and crystals limited their range of motion. Mikael peered closer in the deep river to make out the faint glow of other crystals. Mikael frowned. Even with the extra light from the crystals, he could not make out any small fish or any aquatic animals. Not a good sign.

"Let's keep moving," Mikael urged.

The passage way opened up wide, leading them into subterranean area. As the water descended down, it split into several dozen different directions. Small cracks and holes peppered the cave floor, most likely leading to different parts of the maze. Along the ground were a variety of more crystals and small, red crabs crawling over the minerals.

Mikael landed, carefully avoiding the small crustaceans. He crouched down low to look for any clues for which path the Abaddon took. He searched for any signs of a demon passing through. Claw-marks? Footprints? Broken crystals?

Nothing, he thought. He saw no signs of any creature passing by recently. Mikael scooped up some water and splashed his face. He didn't want to go home empty handed. *Especially with how scared poor Ava has been,* he thought. His heart clenched at the thought. He rubbed his face vigorously as he wondered about his next move. He stared blankly at the water, weighing his limited options. Disgruntled, he smacked the water.

"Hey!" Elijah whispered harshly. "Do not disturb the water, remember!"

Elijah landed on a large crystal opposite to him. Mikael grunted as something caught his eye. A lighter type of glow, not the blue glow of the crystals, but of something else. Mikael ducked his face under the water to see a blazing, white portal. A portal underwater in the Maze of Uncertainty!

Mikael pulled his face above the water. "Found something!" he yelled at Elijah, who jumped. "Found a portal at the bottom of the waterfall. The Abaddon must have used it to escape."

"Great," Elijah began, "We can go after it."

Just then, a bloodcurdling scream pierced the air around them. Hairs on the back of Mikael's neck lifted at the shriek. Elijah swirled around to the opening the scream came from. Both of their wings flared wide.

"My son." Elijah's face paled, and his hands trembled.

Mikael looked down at the portal once. He gritted his teeth before jerking away from the water. "Let's go!"

He zoomed down the tunnel where the scream had come from, praying they made it there in time. Elijah, for the first time, kept up with him, frantically flapping his wings, and clawing his way through the maze.

"Hang on, son!" Elijah yelled.

It was every parent's worst nightmare.

Mikael pushed his wings harder.

Bubbles floated up to the surface, taking away the air Noah desperately needed. The silence of being underwater created a drastic contrast to his screaming thoughts. His lungs burned fiercely. Noah convulsed as his body attempted to get oxygen. A tentacle gripped his left leg, while another began to wrap around his waist to drag him down further. Noah stabbed at the tentacle with his free hand. He had made the wise decision to draw his sword before he, Zewal, and Tariel swam further upstream.

A low rumble rippled through the water as the tentacle retreated, sending three other tentacles in its wake. Noah scrambled toward the surface, critically needing air. He broke the surface gasping for all of two seconds, before being dragged down again. Darkness and silence encased him once more.

Noah stabbed the creature again, this time swimming downward to cut further along the appendage. Another rumble echoed in the water. Noah searched frantically, adrenaline pumping through him. He spotted Zewal's pale wings against the contrast of the dark water. He swam for him.

Zewal was dragged down at the same time as Noah. They had just helped Tariel up a large crystal to rest when this creature attacked. It pulled them from the shore and away from the surface. They barely had any time to breathe before going underwater.

Now, Zewal was losing his battle against these large tentacles. Zewal's eyes rolled into the back of his head, and his body went limp right as Noah reached him. Noah cut the tentacles coming from the bottom, slicing through. This time, a shriek ran through the water, but Noah was too busy hauling Zewal's entangled body up to the surface. His body and lungs burned. His body moved like it was in mud instead of water as exhaustion set in. *Come on!* he thought.

He broke the surface, gasping again. He pulled Zewal's head up to the surface as he struggled toward the shoreline where Tariel screamed. Noah turned to see the tentacle monster emerge to the surface just behind him. A large, bulbous head lifted with two large eyes along its side.

Noah paled. A kraken.

The worst possible outcome had happened.

"SWIM!" Tariel screeched at him.

Noah carried Zewal on his back as he paddled to the shore.

Tariel screamed again as she lifted her hand at the kraken. Her eyes darkened around her eye sockets as she drained the kraken of strength. The kraken groaned as it lifted a tentacle sluggishly to swipe at Noah. He dragged Zewal, while everything in his body burned. His lungs still gasped for air, while his arms and legs ached. The shore looked far away, but he had to keep going.

Tariel shook with effort as she sapped the energy from the monster. Her powers waned. The kraken smacked one of its tentacles dangerously close to where Noah swam. Its accuracy was getting better. Noah tried to move faster, but his limbs were too exhausted.

"No!" Tariel screamed.

Noah looked up to see a large tentacle descending toward them. He closed his eyes, accepting there was nothing more he could do. The sound of scraping metal made Noah open his eyes to see a large figure and bat-like wings zoom by. For a half second, Noah thought he saw Arick flying in the air, killing the monster. After a few moments, he realized it was Mikael slicing up their opponent. Mikael moved so fast that Noah didn't see him cut the tentacle; it was suddenly split open, spewing black blood everywhere. The kraken screeched and curled in on itself. It began to retreat back underwater, but Mikael grabbed one of its limbs. Noah refused to peel his eyes away as Mikael hauled the huge kraken out of the water and slammed it against the crystal wall. Over and over and over again.

The kraken must have weighed tons, but Mikael made it look easy.

Something gripped Noah's collar tightly, sending him into another panic.

"Noah," a familiar, deep voice ceased Noah's scrambling.

He looked up to see his father's, eyes wide with worry as Elijah hauled him and Zewal out of the water. Elijah quickly flew over to Tariel. Her sunken eyes followed Zewal's still form as his father put them both down.

Elijah put his hands over Zewal's chest, just above his heart. His hands glowed with his healing ability. Tariel scrambled over to where they laid; her limbs trembled with each step. After a few long seconds, Zewal spewed water out of his mouth. Elijah turned Zewal on his side, while he coughed up water. Still panting for air, Noah's wings and shoulders relaxed. His body melted into the ground with exhaustion.

He turned his head to the side to see the kraken on the other side of the river, limp. Black blood painted the crystal wall behind it as Mikael hovered in the air. The kraken was no longer their problem, but how did Mikael and his father get there? Why were they here? As the questions started to enter his head, Noah was yanked up by the collar. Now face-to-face with his father, who looked enraged, Noah gave a sheepish grin.

"Long time no see," he croaked out.

Elijah released a long exhale as his eyes narrowed.

"What, in all of the realms, are you doing here?" Elijah shook Noah slightly.

"I could ask the same of you!" Noah replied defensively. "What are you and Mikael doing here?"

"That is not important." Mikael's deep voice drew his attention. "What matters now is that you children hurry home."

Out of the corner of his eye, Noah saw Tariel and Zewal bristle at Mikael's statement.

"We can't go home. Not yet, at least," Noah started. Another yank at his collar.

"*You* damn well are going back home!" Elijah nearly yelled. "After this reckless stunt you pulled."

"I *need* to do this!" Noah tried to free himself from his father's grip. "Arick needs help and—"

"That does not involve you putting your life in danger like this!" Elijah argued. He finally released Noah, standing up. With his hands on his hips, Elijah moved closer to the river.

"You were almost taken from us just now," Elijah said softly as his wings trembled. His back was still turned to Noah.

Noah realized, with some guilt, where his father's fear came from. He saw Noah being take away from him just like Ava. Noah remembered how crushed his parents were when Ava was taken. He knew how scared and depressed they became after what happened.

But that was years ago. Ava was still alive, and so was he.

He clenched his fists as he stood up.

"I am my own person, Father," Noah said softly. "And I am not afraid."

"Well, I am." Elijah turned to look at him.

"And that is something you have to deal with. Not me," Noah fired back.

A silence followed that stretched between them, widening the gap. Noah looked at his father with new eyes. Eyes that saw how much fear and anger had dictated his family's life.

Fear that had caused Ava to panic at the thought of telling her parents of her pregnancy. Fear that kept him and Charlotte locked up in the house for years on end, causing them to miss out on life. Fear pushed Arick to drink himself to oblivion because he saw a world where no one would accept him.

Noah was tired of this cycle. He was done with it.

A cough broke the silence first. Noah moved his gaze to Mikael standing by the tunnel they came through.

"We need to keep moving," Mikael said firmly. "The kraken is not the only thing in the water down here. Come, we will show you the way we came to lead you outside."

Tariel helped her brother up. Their wings stretched wide before they lifted themselves into the sky.

"Son," Elijah started. He paused as if he couldn't get any more words out.

Noah sighed before lifting himself up into the air to follow the tunnel Mikael indicated.

They all flew in silence. Whether that was because no one knew what to say or they wanted to avoid attracting any more attention, Noah did not know. Nor did he care. He still needed answers, but he had failed. His fruitless effort in finding a Seraphim stung at his pride. If he couldn't help his family, how would he ever succeed in helping his people?

Mikael peeked at him from the corner of his eyes, but Noah ignored him. Mikael slowed down enough that he was nearly side by side with him, but Mikael's wings were far too wide to allow it.

"Why were you down here?" Mikael asked firmly.

"I wanted to find answers for Arick," Noah answered. He wasn't in the mood to talk anymore.

Mikael regarded him pensively as they came to an opening. Before him stood a tall waterfall surrounded by glowing crystals. The high ceiling gave Noah a clue as to how deep they truly were in the maze. A large pool of water laid in front of them with glowing crystals laying at what Noah assumed to be the bottom. Tariel landed on one of the crystals nearby. She bent down and picked something up.

"Look," she said softly. In her hand, small, red crabs crawled.

"Put those down!" Zewal cried. He smacked her hand, knocking down the two crabs into the water. "You don't know if they're poisonous or not."

"You didn't have to hit my hand," Tariel grumbled.

Noah watched the crabs sink into the rippling water.

"Come now," Elijah urged behind him. "The way out is just above the waterfall and straight out."

Noah continued to watch the crabs sink. The water glowed blue from the crystals, but as the crabs descended, the glow turned white. Noah leaned in closer, curiosity piqued. There, at the bottom, was a distinct, white glowing oval, one that resembled a portal.

A portal.

Noah jumped up. A portal that could lead him to a Seraphim! He still had a chance.

"A portal is down there at the bottom of the pool!" Noah shouted.

Zewal and Tariel's heads turned down, but his father grimaced at his proclamation. Mikael did not appear surprised in the slightest. Noah swiveled his head back and forth, looking at them.

"You knew this?" Noah said slowly.

Mikael gave a small nod, but his eyes were on Elijah.

Noah turned to his father, who sighed.

"We tracked the Abaddon all the way here. We were about to go through the portal when we heard Tariel scream," Elijah explained. He moved closer to Noah. "Please, son, do not follow us into the portal. There is only danger on the other side."

"So, I am to go home and do nothing?" Noah asked. His anger flared again. "How long will you keep trying to keep us locked away?"

His father flinched. "Better that than never seeing you again."

Noah clenched his fists in frustration. How could he convince his father to change his mind? What would it take? He slowly relaxed his hands as a thought came into his mind.

"You said you were tracking an Abaddon. The same Abaddon that attacked Charlotte and Atarah?" he asked.

"Yes," his father said hesitantly.

"But you don't know where the portal leads to?"

Silence. That answered his question.

"Then I am coming with," Noah said firmly.

Elijah's wings flared. "No—"

"I was not asking." Noah flared his wings out, determined. "I am well of age and the heir to the Raphael Clan. I know the risk, and it is my life to live. I am coming with, so I can fulfill my own mission." He glanced at Zewal and Tariel. "Thank you for coming this far with me. I can't ask you to go any farther."

"There's no need to ask." Zewal finally tore his eyes away from the portal. "We have the same goal in mind."

"We are all going together," Tariel said softly, leaning over a crystal to peer into the water.

"That settles it," Mikael said as he hovered directly over the portal.

Mikael looked to Elijah's stricken face with sympathy. Something silent passed between the two of them. Something Noah couldn't name, but a change had taken place.

"Having children is never easy." Mikael curled in his wings and dove into the water.

None of them hesitated. They dove into the unknown.

Chapter 10

Atarah grimaced as she slowly opened her eyes. Her eyes protested the interruption of her dreamless sleep, but years of training forced them open. She opened her eyes to see Charlotte by her bedside.

After they drank the serum in the cavern with the rangers, they left the underground. The dark tunnel they had run down led to the outside. The outdoor human world, that is. Once above ground, they ran out into a bright, wide-open space. The hot weather was the first thing Atarah had noticed. The sun sent wave after wave of blistering heat down upon them. The landscape around them consisted of rocks, sand, and the occasional withered-looking plant.

"Where are we?" Atarah had asked Flynn yesterday.

"We are in the Mojave Desert," he had answered. "Get ready for we have a long run ahead of us."

A long run was an understatement. The team of rangers split into two. Half went south, while the other half went north. She, along with the other Archs, went north with Flynn. Imani led the other group south. They agreed on some rendezvous point that Atarah had never heard of called "Las Vegas." Since they parted with the others, all they had done was run through the desert. Most rangers had a light backpack with the necessities, but that was it. In their group, there were about ten rangers, not including Flynn. They all seemed... not unfriendly... for the most part.

They ran in the desert sun for hours. They only stopped when it looked like Charlotte and Gabriel were about to pass out. Atarah had never seen such a vibrant shade of red on Charlotte before. Even back in the Spirit realm when they rode horseback, she did not appear as exhausted. Flynn said it was because of the loss of their wings. The wings helped cool down their body temperatures better and helped circulate the blood efficiently. Flynn explained that their bodies may feel different for a while and that they would feel the effects even more when they were exercising.

She felt it more this morning. Her throbbing body forced her attention back to the present as she tried to focus on Charlotte's face. Exhaustion seemed to wrap itself tightly around Atarah. Her back felt so sore, she hesitated to move against the pain. She groaned as she tried to sit up. Her whole body ached; even her fingers hurt. Charlotte's tired face finally came into focus. Her eyes were sunken in slightly from exhaustion. Her body shook with effort to do even the smallest task.

"Morning," Atarah murmured.

Charlotte gave a weak smile. Last night, their 'campsite' consisted of a tarp that was laid out and a few blankets. Sleeping under the stars was great and all, until you realized just how uncomfortable it was.

"They are getting ready," Charlotte said softly. She sat up from the spot where she laid and glanced around.

The rangers were already up and moving. One with light brown hair and an athletic frame was cooking breakfast for everyone. Atarah believed his name was Jose. Other rangers were either packing up the blankets or passing out water.

Atarah glanced around for Ben and her brother. Her eyes settled on Ben's stiff form as he walked over to them. He had a hand behind his head, rubbing his neck.

"That was the roughest sleep I've had in a long time." Ben groaned as he approached them. He crouched down to Atarah with concern.

Her heart flipped in her chest as she peered into his eyes.

"How are you doing?" Ben asked softly. As if he was truly concerned.

Despite his fatigue, he still managed to look handsome. His hair was tousled, eyes were red, and none of them had showered in days, but she thought he was the most attractive being ever.

Atarah gripped her blanket tightly against the pain of feelings that came into her heart. She noticed how much Ben was going out of his way to watch after her. All the times he looked at her with concern. The times when he hovered close by her side. It hurt because she so desperately wanted to trust him, but wasn't sure if she could.

"I am fine," she murmured.

Ben frowned at her. She loved that he didn't press more on her feelings, while she still tried to figure them out on her own.

"How are you doing, Charlotte?" Ben said after a moment.

Charlotte glanced between them before answering.

"Definitely not the best sleep, but I'll live." Charlotte offered another weak smile.

Ben nodded before turning back to her.

"We are almost to our destination, apparently," Ben said. "After you two went to sleep, I asked Flynn some more about what we are doing and what our plan is."

Atarah sat up straighter. This she was interested in. She wanted to know how the Watchers could help them fight against that Luciferian. How did this all connect? All the questions she had been too exhausted to ask last night came to the surface. Atarah paused for a moment.

"Wait," Atarah said.

Ben froze. His eyes fixated on her with an intensity that made her heart race.

"We should wait until we gather with everyone for breakfast. It is best if everyone hears what you've learned, then we can ask our own questions to Flynn too," she explained.

Ben gave a small grin and nodded.

A loud bang alerted everyone's attention.

They all turned to see Jose banging on a pot.

"Breakfast is ready!" he yelled.

Ben offered his hand to help her up. Atarah hesitated, but took his hand. Charlotte kept sending Atarah small grins as if she was amused by them. Atarah ignored her.

They all gathered around the makeshift fire pit and began to pass around the food. Arick sat across from her, along with his three comrades, while Atarah sat with Charlotte, Ben, and Gabriel. Today's breakfast consisted of oats. No seasoning. Just boiled water and oats. They had limited bowls, so they had to share the available bowls. Atarah took a bite of the oatmeal and forced herself to swallow. It was lumpy and incredibly bland. *Sand at least has a salty flavor,* Atarah thought. She hadn't realized that the frozen expression on her face gave her away.

"It's okay, princess." Flynn sat down across from her. "I feel the same way. Who put Jose on breakfast duty? He's the worst cook we have."

"Hey!" Jose protested.

He grinned as he put a hand on his chest. "I am offended. I work and slave all morning for you all to have breakfast, and this is the thanks I get?" He threw up his hands. "Whatever happened to gratitude in this world?" he said mockingly.

Several of the rangers laughed alongside him. Atarah couldn't help grinning.

"Whatever happened to the good cooks in the world?" Arick jeered, causing a bout of laughter across the camp.

Jose laughed, while others joined in the camaraderie. Atarah took this chance to scarf down her breakfast quickly. She tried to do it fast enough that she could ignore the dry, bland flavor until she had nothing left.

"It can't be that bad if she can eat it all?" Jose tried to defend himself.

Everyone laughed, while Atarah took huge gulps of water to try to wash it down. Atarah set her container down firmly and shuddered. She looked up at everyone.

"Next time, I'll cook," she said.

Everyone laughed again as she refilled her water container. Flynn had eaten his portion by the time Atarah questioned him.

"So, what's next?" Atarah asked. Her voice had not been loud, but everyone heard her anyway.

Everyone turned to look at Flynn, all as curious as her.

"We aren't too far away from a Watcher. Once we reach the Watcher, the plan is to strike up a deal with him. If he helps us against the Luciferian, we will advocate for him in the Spirit realm."

"If not?" Charlotte asked from where she sat beside Atarah.

Flynn looked at her. "Then we find another Watcher."

"Is that why the other group traveled south?" Atarah asked. Her eyes stayed on Flynn.

"They went south as a backup plan. Not many spiritual beings would want to clash against a Luciferian, so they ventured to find some insurance." Flynn looked around from Arick, Ben, to Charlotte, and then Atarah last.

"How would the Watcher help us exactly?" Gabriel asked from beside Charlotte. His black hair flopped in front of his eyes, giving him a tousled look. He had become less uptight since they first arrived in the human realm.

"The Watcher can move to and from the different realms easier than we can, especially the demon realm. With no real form, they pass through quite easily. They could provide a wealth of information and be good spies." Flynn stared at everyone. "If possible, we want to see if they could possess the Luciferian long enough to transport him. In addition to the wealth of knowledge they possess."

"Transport him where?" Arick's face appeared pale.

Flynn frowned. "Hopefully to your father, Mikael. Also, it wouldn't hurt if he had a good bit of backup." He opened his arms wide to indicate them. "We would join him in taking down the Luciferian."

"Do you know where our dad is?" Atarah asked. She couldn't help the relief slipping into her voice at the mention of her father. Flynn shrugged.

Flynn shrugged, "That's Luke's part."

"How is Luke going to locate him?" Arick asked. "Is he going into the Spirit realm?"

Flynn shrugged again. "When Luke says he will do something, we all know it will be done."

"Is the Head of the Michael Clan really that powerful?" another ranger asked.

Atarah glanced at the ranger. She was fairly tall but muscular. She had snow white hair and green eyes. She must have come from the Uriel Clan to have such coloring. Atarah wondered what element she controlled.

Flynn gave a humorless laugh. "Mikael may be the only one who can truly give this Luciferian a hard time in a fight." Flynn peered at Arick and Atarah with a question swimming in his eyes.

If Atarah had her wings, she knew they would flare slightly at the challenge Flynn silently gave. Arick's gaze stayed down and he pursed his lips together.

"We will take this Luciferian down," Atarah said confidently.

"Shouldn't Mikael be the one tracking down the Luciferian?" the ranger with white hair spoke again.

"What makes you think he's not already?" Atarah challenged.

Flynn sighed and glanced at the ranger. "Sahra, she is right. We sent word about the Luciferian showing up in the human world to Mikael. So, he and the other Arch Heads are aware. None of them can ignore a spiritual being this powerful."

"Do you know what the Arch Heads are planning, then?" Ben asked from beside her.

Flynn frowned slightly as everyone turned back to him. "I do not. But Luke does."

"When do we meet back up with Luke?" Jose asked this time.

Flynn's lips turned up in a small smile. "Depends on how quickly we can complete our part of the job."

"So, we are to complete our part of the job without knowing what others are doing?" Gabriel asked.

"No, we are to trust others to do their part," Flynn said sharply. "Just like they trust us to get this deal with the Watcher."

"And if we can't?" Sahra said softly.

"Then we trust our other teammates to do their part," Flynn replied.

"Ah," Ben said, understanding before the rest of them. "The insurance."

"Exactly." Flynn nodded. "After we do our part, then Luke will tell us what comes next."

All the rangers nodded. Flynn focused on Atarah, waiting for her response. Atarah gave a small nod. They would follow along with Luke's plan.

"Good." Flynn stood. "It's time to move out, then."

With that, everyone went into motion. Everyone began to pack and get ready for another day of running. Atarah only carried a canteen for her water and the clothes on her back. She was grateful to have changed out of her previously torn clothes. The clothes she had been in when fighting an Abaddon and traveling in the human realm were so dirty that no other color but brown appeared on her. One of the rangers had given her a pair of gray capri leggings with a soft, short-sleeve black shirt the night before. She had never felt better. Even though she had yet to shower, the feeling of new clothes on her was welcome.

She fastened her canteen across her body and turned to check on Charlotte. Charlotte had also received some new clothes. She wore black capri leggings with a tight-fitting, green shirt that brought out the hazel color of her eyes. She was lacing up her running shoes when Atarah glanced at her. She glanced around for Ben to see him doing the same, but he was looking back at her. They had all been given some new clothes.

Ben wore an athletic shirt that showed nearly all of his muscles with some running shorts and shoes all in black. Everything he did looked graceful and at ease except for a tightness around his eyes. His eyes showed Atarah how he was truly doing. Once he was done with his shoes, he approached her.

"Keep looking at me like that and I'll begin to think you care for me again," Ben tried to say lightly, but sorrow still coated his words. He lightly touched her cheek.

"I don't... dislike you anymore," Atarah said awkwardly.

Ben gave a small smile. "That's a relief." Ben gazed deeply into her eyes. "Atarah," he said softly. "I want to explain why I did what I did. Before we came to the human realm."

Atarah shook her head as her chest tightened in pain. She didn't want to be reminded of his betrayal. It hurt too much.

"No, please listen," Ben pleaded. He took a step closer, his brown eyes imploring. "I care about you, Atarah." His voice was strong and did not waver in the slightest. His gaze was so intense she felt like he could see her soul. Atarah hugged herself to keep herself together. She wanted to believe Ben so badly it hurt.

"I know it didn't seem like it back in Antiqua, but I promise—"

"Promise what?" Atarah interrupted, some bitterness entering her voice. She turned away from him to avoid his gaze.

"Promise not to scheme or force me into a marriage? Promise to be honest with me?" she continued.

Ben grabbed her arm and turned her around, so she had no choice but to look at him.

"I promise all that and more," Ben said softly. His brown eyes bored into hers. "I told you before that I want to earn your trust."

She could feel tears welling in her eyes. She closed her eyes to keep them from falling. Ben's arms encircled around her in an embrace. She almost pushed him away. Almost.

A ranger named Eshu who had a tall, thin build with coily, black hair called out to draw their attention. "Time to move out!" he yelled across camp. His brown complexion glistened against the sun.

Many of the others were already packed and ready to head out. Charlotte hovered a little bit away. Enough distance for privacy, but not too far away that she couldn't reach her.

"I mean it, Atarah. I will explain everything when we can get a little more privacy," Ben said softly as he drew in close to her ear.

His lips brushed against her temple in the lightest of kisses before drawing back. Atarah's heart thumped rapidly in her chest, while tears filled her eyes. Her heart and body said yes, but her head said caution.

"Oh," Ben paused. "I almost forgot."

Ben lifted up both hands. He pinched the tip of his finger on his left hand and lifted. Like a curtain, gloves materialized off his hand. *The gloves!* It took Atarah a moment to recognize the gloves she had grabbed from Chrysi Poli. The gloves that revealed truth in others and also oneself. Last time, she had worn them for a few hours, and she had been overwhelmed by her emotions. Ben had been wearing them this whole time. *For days.*

"I'm sorry I kept these for so long. I wanted to look inward at myself with my feelings for you." Ben stared at Atarah as he handed the gloves over to her. "I can say without a shadow of a doubt, you mean the universe and all of the realms combined to me, Atarah." His eyes shined brightly with an emotion she could finally identify.

Love.

Before she could do anything foolish, Ben retreated to grab his own light pack. Atarah turned away to see Charlotte right next to her. Atarah stuffed the gloves into her small pack.

"You all right?" she asked softly. Her bright hazel eyes flickered between her and Ben's retreating form.

"Yeah." Atarah nodded numbly. Ben's reveal that he had the gloves this whole time still rocked her to her core. "I just don't know if I could ever trust him again."

In her heart, she still loved him.

Charlotte pursed her lips and looked back at her.

"It couldn't hurt to hear him out," Charlotte said quietly. "We don't know his side of the story or what pressure is on his shoulders from his family."

Atarah shook her head. She didn't want to talk about Ben anymore. It was too raw.

"Have you thought about what will happen when we go back to the Spirit realm?" Atarah asked.

Charlotte visibly paled, and her hands shook a little as she answered. "I don't want to talk about it."

Atarah nodded, understanding. However, she did want to look out for Charlotte.

"You are always welcome in my home, Charlotte. It is rough terrain and full of stubborn, meat-headed angels." She grinned as she thought about home. "But it is good."

They had begun to line up with the rangers and were about to jog before Charlotte replied.

"I think I... I may like that." Her voice was hesitant and soft. Her eyes were staring ahead, unseeing.

Atarah wondered what else happened with Charlotte and her mother growing up to cause such a fearful reaction.

A movement to Charlotte's left caught Atarah's eye. Gabriel stood beside Charlotte, glancing down at her with concern. Another emotion swam in his eyes, but Atarah couldn't place it.

Gabriel saw Atarah had caught him staring at Charlotte and blushed. He gave a half shrug of '*What are you looking at?*' while flushed with embarrassment. Atarah gave the smallest of smiles at Gabriel. He cared about Charlotte. Enough that he didn't back down when Atarah challenged him. *Good,* she thought. Charlotte deserved someone who was willing to face anything for her, even her violent best friend.

They all took off running. The sun had risen well over the horizon now. The day was not yet hot enough to begin scorching them, but it would not matter, for Charlotte would heal any burns before they could even register them. Atarah almost laughed as another movement caught her eye. Galvin, one of Arick's soldiers, fell in line behind Charlotte, closely. Charlotte was still not as physically fit as the rest of them, so she often fell to the back. Atarah stayed with her yesterday, but this time Gabriel and Galvin both decided to fall back with them. Charlotte blushed briefly at the nonverbal challenges the males sent to one another. Atarah actually began to laugh quietly. Knowing her friend, Atarah giggled at how embarrassed Charlotte was in that situation. Charlotte had been so sheltered, she felt awkward around most males. While Charlotte grew anxious under the glares of the two males vying for her attention, Atarah's thoughts turned elsewhere.

She stared at Ben's running form in front of her and wondered what his life had been like. She realized how little she knew about his past. Charlotte had not been the only one sheltered, she thought grimly. She only knew the overall basics of each region, but nothing in detail. She thought back to their time in Chrysi Poli. The reserved manner of its people. The hungry look in their eye for knowledge and secrets. In the Michael Clan, they valued strength. In the Selaphiel Clan, they valued learning and discovery. What must it have been like for Ben growing up? What led up to the moment when they met? She thought back to when they had met in Elijah's—

Atarah almost stumbled forward.

Of course! she thought.

Their 'plan' was already in motion before they had met. She wondered what Ben thought of her in the moments before they met. Even still, she thought back to how he looked surprised when they had arrived in Silva. She wondered what had gone through his mind then. She wondered what her parents would think of him.

A bump on her shoulder drew her out of her thoughts.

"You're going to run into a cactus if you let your mind wander," Arick said easily. He was barely breathing hard. His hair was starting to grow out again, and his black curls bounced with each step. He acted completely at ease.

Atarah snorted and rolled her eyes. To which Arick laughed.

"All right. If you run into a cactus, I am just gonna point at you and laugh at your own stupidity."

"And if *you* run into a cactus—"

"Eh, I probably wouldn't feel it," Arick cut her off arrogantly.

"That's not fair," Atarah complained. They jogged side by side now.

Arick's tight, fitted, white shirt shined against his brown skin. He wasn't sweating yet. While he looked at ease, she knew better. Arick had been more withdrawn since she had last seen him. Even though he talked with others and engaged with jokes, Atarah noted a heaviness in his tone that had not been there before. While he physically looked fine, he behaved differently. He was hesitant, unsure about himself and everything he did. She looked at him as if she could spot the reason for this change. Nothing out of sorts. His steps faltered under her scrutiny.

"Trying to plot my demise, little cricket?"

"Plotting an emotional ambush actually," Atarah replied, still regarding Arick.

Even when running, his shoulders tensed up.

"Please don't." Arick groaned.

"What's up with you? Why are you being a wimp?" Atarah said with the bluntness of a younger sibling.

Arick groaned and tried to speed up. Atarah kept up with him.

"Don't try to avoid me," Atarah huffed, while sprinting to keep up with him. She was vaguely aware that they were now leading the group. If they kept at this pace, they would be well ahead of everyone.

"Well?" Atarah panted. "Does this have anything to do with the Luciferian?"

"Dammit, Atarah!" Arick grunted. "Can't you take a hint? I don't want to talk about it."

"But you need to—"

"I don't need to do anything!" Arick nearly yelled. He slowed down his pace a little.

Atarah gave him a moment before speaking.

"What's going on, big guy?" Atarah asked more gently. They were now at a jogging pace rather than sprinting.

Arick sighed.

"I don't… know how I feel," Arick began. "Matthew is my real father, yet—"

"Matthew?" Atarah said, jarred by the name. She had forgotten he had a name. She kept referring to him as the Luciferian or monster.

Arick grimaced. "Yet he's—not good," Arick continued.

Atarah pondered in silence for a moment while they ran.

"What happened after you left Ventus with Noah?" Atarah asked, redirecting for a moment.

Arick's shoulders relaxed a little, and the tension in his face loosened.

"Noah and I traveled south through Aquam Caput and the Vallis region. We saw nothing but hot desert and desolated cities."

"And after that?" Atarah pressed. "What is Mortem like? The Azrael angels? What are they like?"

Arick huffed a laugh, and his eyes brightened.

"We met Zewal and his sister Tariel. They are tall, lanky angels who have the most unusual hair." Arick's voice became lighter in tone. "Zewal and their father, Sewall, have a dry sense of humor, and Tariel is shy but tough as nails." Arick had a small smile on his lips at the mention of her name. "They have this incredible power that weakens their opponent in different ways. Most are scared of them, but I think they're just different."

"You seemed to have really bonded with them."

Arick frowned slightly and looked at her.

"When you were first taken to the human realm, I got so angry that I lost control of my powers," Arick confessed. "I destroyed the entire garden area before I even realized I had lost it. Luckily, Tariel was there, and she was able to use her powers to weaken me so I didn't hurt anyone, but—" Arick looked away from her. "I felt nothing. No empathy, no hatred… nothing. My powers just unleashed. It was like watching someone else control my body, while my mind was numb." Arick sighed. "That moment is what scares me the most. Not my power being uncontrollable, but the lack of feeling in that moment. I didn't care enough to even try to control my powers. Like a ghost tethered to a body, but the ghost doesn't care about the attachment."

"You're scared of losing control?" Atarah glanced back to check on the others. They were far away. Maybe they should stop and let them catch up? Atarah slowed down, and Arick followed.

"I am scared of feeling that apathy again. At that moment, everything was meaningless…" Arick stared at her as they came to a stop. "And it felt *so* unbelievably comforting. I wanted to hold onto that apathy because it made me feel invincible."

They paused and waited for the group to catch up with them. She hadn't realized how far ahead they had gotten until she had looked back.

"You're ashamed?" Atarah said quietly. She had asked that as a question, but as soon as the words were out of her mouth, she knew they were true.

Arick nodded grimly. "I had just found out about Matthew. It is one thing to hear the story of Matthew, how he hurt our mother and escaped, but... I *felt* like his son at that moment." Arick shuddered. "When I felt it in my bones—the truth—I feel too ashamed to be anything else but his son."

Atarah cocked her head to the side and squinted at her brother. The sun was now blazing down on them with no cloud in sight. She could see the heat waves move across the land, scorching as they went along.

Sweat dripped down her back from the heat and the exertion of the run. Atarah stood quietly as she took in what he said. She didn't know what that felt like to question who you were. However, she knew what it felt like to be an outsider looking in.

"An outsider?" a voice hissed from behind her.

She whirled around, fists raised and ready to fight. Arick jumped back, drawing his dagger.

They both scanned the area and saw nothing. The small hairs on the back of her neck stood up. The air suddenly felt colder, despite the desert heat from before. Something was here with them.

"Who's there?" Atarah asked.

She continued to scan the area for anything strange. The others still appeared far away, still trying to catch up to them. Shouldn't the rangers have reached them by now?

"Outsider..." the voice hissed in her ear again.

She jerked her head around. Nothing but a few red rocks and sand. The wind swirled around them, carrying a foul stench, a smell of rotting flesh. She and Arick both winced at the aroma.

"Another outsider has come to join me," it said.

Arick stood back-to-back with her, cautious of their surroundings.

"Who are you?" Arick said.

"Show yourself!" Atarah demanded at the same time.

The wind shuddered as if chuckling at them.

The breeze calmed for a few seconds before the voice came back.

A harsh laugh echoed around them.

"Foolish kids you are." It laughed darkly. "If you don't know when you are in the presence of a Watcher, you should just tuck your tails and go home."

They froze. *A Watcher! They had found one!* Atarah glanced back at their comrades and still saw them running. They didn't appear to be any closer. They should have at least gotten closer. Did the Watcher have something to do with this?

"Yes, child," the soft voice said. "Since you are within my presence, both of you are in a slightly different... dimension."

"Dimension?" Arick asked hesitantly.

The Watcher sighed. "My cursed state," it sneered. "A place between the realms where time and space are altered. A place where I will never be allowed a physical form, forever detached... unless you two help me."

"Help you how?" Atarah slowly lowered her fists.

She hadn't been prepared to bargain with the Watcher. She needed to think of a plan carefully. Flynn knew the dynamic pieces better than she did. But he was far off in the distance, running to them but not moving forward. He wouldn't reach them while they were with the Watcher.

It scoffed at her. "You truly are an ignorant child. I want a more physical form, and your people want information on

Matthew the Luciferian. It is a simple exchange, kid."

"How do you know what we want?" Atarah questioned. She glanced at Arick, unsure. Why was this Watcher so eager to help them? Did it have an ulterior motive?

"You angels are never hard to figure out. Even if I hadn't heard your whispers and fears, it would be so easy to predict what you would do next," the voice mocked her. "The Luciferian easily showed up in the human realm and sent the rangers into a buzz. One does not simply walk between realms. It takes tremendous power."

"How is he able to open a portal then? He opened one in the Coal Mountains and another one in the human world like it was nothing. How?" Atarah asked urgently.

"Tsk, tsk, tsk," the voice said. "This is a bargain, darling. Information has a price here."

Atarah groaned in frustration. The Watcher was right; they had come here to bargain.

"What exactly do you want?" Arick asked calmly.

"Ah, the Luciferian's son," the voice cooed. "I will help you defeat this Luciferian in exchange for a body, specifically a Gabriel angel's body."

"But—" Atarah bit her tongue to stay silent.

They didn't have a body to spare; the Watcher must know this. Arick pondered the Watcher's ridiculous demands. They would never turn a body over to be possessed. How were they supposed to bargain with this creature?

"I want something else," Arick said.

"Oh?" the Watcher replied. "You aren't curious about your father, halfling?"

"No," Arick said softly. He paused. "I'll give you my body in exchange for something."

"What?! No!" Atarah yelled. "You will not be possessed, Arick." She turned to her brother. "I told you before and I'll say it again, you are not evil!"

The Watcher grew silent, and the wind stilled.

"It is my body, Atarah. You do not get to decide for me." Arick turned his back to her. "What do you say, Watcher? Do you want an exchange?"

"You are a strange angel…" The Watcher's voice sounded surprised. "What is it you want?"

"I want you to tell me your name, Watcher," Arick replied.

Atarah was stunned. His body in exchange for a simple name! A useless name! How could that possibly help them? She was about to protest, but the Watcher cut her off.

The Watcher burst out in laughter. The wind swirled around them, blowing sand to and fro. Atarah brought her arms around her head to shield herself against the sand.

"A surprise! Oh, what a surprise," the voice jeered. "It has been thousands of years since I have been surprised by something."

The Watcher's laugh died down to a chuckle. A swirl of sand stood tall before Arick.

"It has been even longer since someone has cared enough to ask for my name. I have never felt more… solid. I am feeling generous. In exchange for your body, I shall give you my name and help your people against the Luciferian." The tornado of sand moved closer to Arick. "Do we have a deal?"

Arick gave a small, sad grin. "It is a done deal."

"No!" Atarah shouted.

She moved to grab onto Arick, but she was too late. The sand swirled around them in a massive sandstorm. A burst of hot air greeted her hand as she tried to grasp him, but there was nothing there.

"Atarah!" a voice yelled.

Slowly, as the sand died down, she turned to see the rangers had finally reached them. Ben sprinted toward her with concern, almost panic, on his face. Flynn was right behind him as Ben cupped her face.

"Are you okay? It looked like you were in a sandstorm." Ben's eyes frantically searched the rest of her body for injuries.

She gently took his hands away from her face. "I am fine, I promise." She looked at Flynn. "It's Arick, though. He—"

She turned to see Arick standing behind her. Arick lifted his hands as if in wonder. She approached him slowly.

"Arick? Is that you?" she asked cautiously.

Arick stared her, his golden eyes taking in the others who'd finally caught up. All the rangers made it to them and now regarded him, apprehensive.

"I'm... still me," Arick said softly. "I thought..." His voice drifted off.

Atarah moved right up to him and punched him with her full force. He doubled over, mouth agape as if trying to gasp for breath.

"You're so stupid!" Atarah bellowed.

Arick gasped, still clutching his stomach. She held back tears of frustration, while Flynn got between her and her brother.

"Woah, woah, woah." Flynn spread his hands out as if to ward her off. "What happened here?"

"You've gotten stronger, Atarah," Arick choked out.

"Arick made the dumbest deal with the devil," Atarah cried.

Ben circled his arms around her, not to hold her back, but to keep her together.

"To be fair, I got a bargain. A two for one if you will," Arick countered, finally straightening up.

"Tell them the whole truth, Arick! No more joking around!"

She grabbed onto Ben's arms for support. He tightened his grip.

"We encountered a Watcher. He knew we were coming," Arick began.

"What did you bargain for?" Flynn glanced between Arick and Atarah.

The others from his team—Galvin, Jared, and Brock—moved closer to him. Suddenly, Arick's face went slack, and his eyes changed. His pupils shifted back and forth quickly as he fell silent.

"What's going on with his eyes?" Jared asked urgently.

Brock and Galvin moved to either side of him, ready to catch him if he fell over.

"It looks like... nystagmus," Charlotte said softly.

"What?" Brock and Jared asked.

"It means uncontrollable, repetitive eye movements," Charlotte explained. "I've seen it mostly with head injuries."

"Clever observation, girl." The voice that came out of Arick was not his own. This one sounded rough. It was the Watcher.

Arick's body turned to Flynn, his pupils still moving back and forth rapidly, but they had a different clarity to them.

"I agreed to help you in exchange for this boy's body," the Watcher explained. "I believe I have some valuable information for you rangers."

"Get out of my brother's body!" Atarah stormed up to the Watcher. Ben was right behind her.

The Watcher laughed. "A deal is a deal, sweetheart." He crouched down to her eye level. "Now do you want this information or not?" he sneered.

Atarah clenched her fists and resisted the urge to punch him again. Well... this time she would punch the Watcher.

"We do need the information, Atarah," Ben whispered in her ear softly.

She paused. She gritted her teeth in frustration because he was right. The deal was already done. There was nothing more she could do about it, except make sure the deal didn't go to waste.

"What is it you know?" Flynn asked, drawing the Watcher's attention.

"The Luciferian has been using a serum to transport his

soldiers and himself."

"A serum?" Flynn asked in amazement.

Arick's head moved up and down as the Watcher from within regarded him.

"It is a black-looking serum. Once they consume it, they can travel through the different realms it seems," the Watcher mused. "As if they were a Gabriel angel."

"This is just the kind of information we needed," Flynn said. "We need to get this knowledge to Luke as soon as possible!" He peered at the Watcher. "Where do they get this serum? What is it made out of?" Flynn fired off questions.

Everyone looked on eager for the answers. This changed everything if demons could transport easily. She needed to warn everyone in the Spirit realm, but more importantly, she needed to tell her father.

The Watcher opened his mouth to answer when another deep voice interrupted.

"It is quite simple really."

Everyone froze. A cold shiver went down Atarah's spine as recognition and fear settled over her. That voice would give her nightmares. Ben grabbed her and pulled her close to him, practically clinging to her as if scared she would be taken. Cautiously, she turned her head—they all did—to see who spoke. There stood Matthew, just a few feet away behind Arick.

Again, she was taken back by how similar he looked to her father. A tall build, maybe even taller than her father, with broad shoulders, black hair, and bright, golden eyes. He clasped his hands together behind his back as he slowly circled around them. He walked like he was on a leisurely stroll. His eyes immediately went to Arick, who still had his back to him.

"It took many years for me to perfect the formula, but in the end, it was simple," Matthew continued when no one said anything. He took his time as he stepped closer to them. He stepped closer to Charlotte, which triggered someone.

Gabriel, who had been a few paces behind Charlotte, darted forward and moved her behind him protectively. Sweat coated his exhausted face, but, somehow, he still managed to glare at Matthew. Those apathetic, golden eyes stared down at Gabriel with mild amusement before turning callous again. He moved like lightning.

Matthew grabbed Gabriel by the throat and lifted him up from the ground. Gabriel choked and jerked to get out of his grip, all in vain. Seeing him choking spurred Atarah and Flynn into action. She lunged to give the hardest kick she could deliver to the back of Matthew's knees, while Flynn moved to attack his arms. Just as they were about to land their blows, Matthew moved.

He moved so fast, it almost looked like he disappeared. Suddenly, he stood next to Arick, still gripping Gabriel by the neck. Everyone circled around him, cutting off any escape.

"As I was saying, it all really is simple," Matthew spoke calmly. He raised Gabriel up to his eye level. "I just needed the blood of a Gabriel angel to create the serum for my army."

Arick finally turned to look at Matthew. His eyes were still and shining brightly with a strong emotion she couldn't decipher. *This* was no doubt her brother back in control. She had never seen such a thunderous expression on Arick's face. Matthew lowered Gabriel to glance back at Arick. He was the only one who stood almost as tall as the Luciferian.

"Hello, son." Matthew gave a chilling grin as he spoke.

Muscles moved in Arick's jaw, but he said nothing. He took a step closer until he was nearly nose-to-nose with Matthew. He grabbed ahold of the hand that gripped Gabriel's throat.

"Let go of him."

Even though his voice was soft, Atarah had never heard her brother sound so enraged.

"I am afraid I can't do that, son." Matthew sighed. "We

need another Gabriel angel to create another batch of the se-rum. You see—"

Matthew's sentence was cut off as Arick delivered a punch so strong the air around them shuddered and vibrated. The ground shook and dust clouded the air as the Luciferian landed a good distance away.

"You do not get to call me son," Arick said softly.

Gabriel spurted and gasped on the ground beside him, on all fours. Charlotte sprinted to him, her hands already glow-ing. Everyone closed in around each other, Flynn in front with his weapons drawn, watching the dust cloud in the distance. The rangers were bracing for a fight. Atarah knelt down where Gabriel was to shake his shoulders.

"Gabriel!" Atarah urged. "Now more than ever we need to get out of here. Open a portal! We need to let the others know how the demons are getting around."

Gabriel still held onto his throat, but nodded all the same. He stretched out a hand and drew a line upward. A bright line appeared before them. Another sound caught Atarah's atten-tion—the sound of thunder. She looked up to see Matthew slam Arick onto the ground and then stomp on him.

"Did you not learn to respect your elders, boy?" Matthew jeered. "No matter. You will be taught soon enough. The cor-rect way."

Matthew turned to them; his eyes narrowed.

No, she thought, *he isn't going after them. He's going af-ter Gabriel.* Atarah scrambled to her feet.

"Ben! Get everyone through that portal NOW!" Atarah yelled.

"Atarah, wait!" Ben shouted, but she was already on the move.

She moved as fast as she could. Her wings ripped out of her back and her powers flooded through her like adrenaline. Matthew watched her approach with little interest. He drew his hand back to hit her, but she was fast enough this time.

She ducked and kicked him as hard as she could. She poured her power into the kick. He was underestimating her, and she would use it to her advantage.

Surprise sprinkled across his features as he was knocked back yards away. She drew her power within herself and brought out her armor. She knew she was no match for him, but she could at least buy the others some time to escape. Arick scrambled to his feet and got in his defensive position. Blood dripped down the side of his face.

"Status?" Atarah barked out. From the sound of impact, Arick most likely had something broken.

"RTF," he choked out. *Ready to fight.* The code they had used during training.

"Aw, well." Matthew chuckled. "Isn't this sweet? You two think you have a chance."

Suddenly, the Luciferian disappeared. The next thing Atarah knew it felt like a battering ram hit her on her right side, knocking her several feet in the air. Her bones snapped upon the impact.

Matthew moved with lightning speed as he delivered the same kick she had given him. Only his was so much stronger. He hadn't even broken a sweat.

Atarah tried to brace herself as his leg struck her first. His leg hit her from the side, sending her flying. She landed on the sand with a dull thud. Her wings cushioned most of the fall. Atarah struggled to stand, but something felt wrong with her side. She glanced down to see her entire left side caved inwards. Her ribs, arm, and hip all looked wrong, and she realized the extent on the damage. That's why she couldn't get up. One hit from him was all it took, and now she was immobile. She heard Arick grunt as he took the impact of Matthew's kick next.

"Atarah!" Ben crouched down and hauled her up.

Adrenaline still pumped through her and kept her body almost numb. Until she was moved, then the pain erupted all around her, nearly drowning her,

"Is everyone out?" she murmured as her consciousness began to fade.

"Almost! Come on, Arick!" Ben bellowed. He moved her through the portal that Gabriel held open.

"Hurry up!" Gabriel yelled. "I can't hold this forever."

Ben moved to take her through the portal.

"Oh no, you don't," Matthew grunted.

He moved so fast none of them saw him coming. He kicked Gabriel down onto the ground so hard, she worried he might be dead. They all heard the snap of Gabriel's arm as he was kicked. Matthew grabbed onto Gabriel's head, lifting him up. His eyes were turning purple and swelling up. The portal began to close as Gabriel lost consciousness.

"I still need you for part of my plan," Matthew said softly to Gabriel's limp form.

"No," she whispered, struggling to remain awake.

Another grunt and thud as Arick tackled Matthew to the ground.

"GO NOW!" Arick shouted. He held Matthew in a body lock.

"No," she whispered again.

Ben hauled Gabriel up with his left arm, while he held her with his right.

"BEN, GO NOW!" Arick yelled again.

Matthew brought both his hands together and slammed them down on his back. Cracks and snaps sounded in the air upon impact. Arick groaned and kept his arm around Matthew.

"No!" Matthew tried to follow them. His face twisted in rage.

Arick didn't let go, but his arms were weakening.

Ben dragged Gabriel and Atarah through the portal just as it closed, and darkness consumed her. The last thing she remembered as the bright, warm light of the portal surrounded her was Arick's arms falling to the ground limp and his blood soaking the sand.

The End

Thank you so much for ordering True Spirit!
If you enjoyed it, please consider leaving a review.
Want more of Atarah and Arick's story? Sign up for my
newsletter to get early access to cover reveals, blurbs
and more!
http://graciemitchell.com

GRACIE MITCHELL

ACKNOWLEDGEMENTS

Thank you so much for continuing to read the stories of Arick, Atarah, Charlotte and so many others. I hope you have enjoyed reading their journey as much as I enjoyed writing their adventures. I am truly grateful for the opportunity to share their stories and I couldn't have done it alone. I express my deepest gratitude to the people below. I want to say thank you to my husband, Malcomn, for cheering me on from the sidelines. You have been my number one fan and supporter. Thank you to my cat Zeus for cuddling by my side as I stay up late to write this book. Thank you for my amazing and supportive family! Love ya'll so much. Every like or share on social media has meant the world

to me. Thank you for everyone who has purchased my book, whether by ebook or by paperback.

Thank you to my editors starting with Connie Dowell for developmental editing and proofreading. Thank you Nichole Heydenburg for both copy and developmental editing. I appreciated all the attention to detail from the feedback given. Thank you every ARC reader for your amazing feedback and hard work.Thank you Terra Hitzing for formatting my book! You are an amazing genius! Thank you Jessica Slater for all of the amazing work you have done for my book cover and design! The cover art looks great! Lastly I want to thank you—the reader. Thank you so much for reading my book and I truly hope you enjoyed this story! If you did, please let me know by leaving a review. I would greatly appreciate it!

GRACIE MITCHELL is a yoga-loving, caffeine addicted writer currently based in Georgia. When she is not working endlessly as an Indie author, she can be found curled up on the couch, with her husband, reading a new book or watching a new tv series. On top of her love to read and write, Gracie enjoys going on adventurous hikes, painting, spending time with her cat and traveling to different countries.

Follow her for more at: https://graciemitchell.com/
Insta: @clanofthearchseries
@gmitchell505

Also by Gracie Mitchell

<u>True Wings (Book 1)</u>

Amazon:
https://a.co/d/eBsedXw

Barnes & Noble:
https://bit.ly/3WllNlY

Apple Books:
https://books.apple.com/us/book/true-wings/id1574054011

Kobo:
https://www.kobo.com/us/en/ebook/true-wings

All other vendors:
https://books2read.com/u/3R82yY

<u>True Spirit (Book 2)</u>

<u>True Strength (Book 3) coming Jan 2023</u>

www.ingramcontent.com/pod-product-compliance
Lightning Source LLC
Chambersburg PA
CBHW030939210726
48290CB00007B/2249